Finding
Juliet

Finding Juliet

Toffee

Srishti
PUBLISHERS & DISTRIBUTORS

SRISHTI PUBLISHERS & DISTRIBUTORS
Registered Office: N-16, C.R. Park
New Delhi – 110 019
Corporate Office: 212A, Peacock Lane
Shahpur Jat, New Delhi – 110 049
editorial@srishtipublishers.com

First published as a digital book by
Juggernaut Books in 2016

Revised version, 2017
First published by
Srishti Publishers & Distributors in 2017

Dedicated to all the Romeos.

Acknowledgements

When a book gets published, the entire credit usually goes to the author of the book. I think it's a bit unfair, because many people contribute to a book, either directly or indirectly. So I take this space to thank all the people who have helped me with this book. Without them, this book wouldn't have happened.

Firstly, thank you Mom, Dad and Sis, for your unconditional love and unflinching support. I am sorry I couldn't be a typical son or brother, as I was too busy chasing my dreams. But I love you more than anyone else and I want to say that I am nothing without you.

Thank you, Swetha, for your unwavering belief that I will become an author someday, especially when nobody else believed.

Thank you, Raghu and Dilip, for correcting my stupid mistakes and for teaching me a million life-lessons. I want to let you know that I am going to make a few more mistakes.

Thank you, Kishore, Vijay, Srikanth, Anil and Suman, for your friendship in college and for choosing to be seen with me in public.

Thank you, Ranjith, for patiently editing my book multiple times and for always being there every time I needed some writing advice.

Thank you, Amulya, Tejaswini, Smruthi, Keerti, Suhasini, Kusuma and Bhavana, for your invaluable feedback and for helping me understand the psychology of women better.

Thank you, Sanjeev Ranjan, for being a great friend, philosopher and guide.

Thank you, Harsh, Shriya, Nikhil, Shubham and Sujata, for helping me through the labyrinth of publishing industry.

Thank you, Abhinash, Arun, Madhu, Sai and Naveen, for making my office-life fun and enjoyable.

Thank you, Dilip and Naresh, for discussing and dissecting the storylines of movies we watched during our school days. I never knew that our silly discussions would one day help me write good books.

Thank you, Binu George sir and Sandhya Reddy ma'am, for teaching English to this boy from a small town.

Thank you, my school friends from CJV and Montessori, for making my childhood memorable. I miss those days all the time.

Thank you, Vijay, Chandu and Ravi, for living the definition of friendship and for being there all the time.

Thank you, Stuti Sharma and Swati Mittal, editors dearest, for bearing with me and for doing a wonderful job at editing the book, making it crisp and perfect.

Thank you, Chiki Sarkar and team, for first publishing the book on Juggernaut's platform as a digital book.

Thank you, Jayanta Kumar Bose da, for creating Srishti publishers and for changing the publishing industry for the better, in your own amazing way.

Special thanks to you Arup Bose, for putting your faith and confidence in my book, for accepting the manuscript for publication and for your support.

Thanks to the entire team at Srishti who work hard to make good books better.

Lastly, thank you 'Toffee', my dear alter ego, for being crazy enough to dream and for being relentless in pursuit of excellence. If it weren't for your insanity, this book wouldn't have been written.

Stint at the hint

'**E**very time I tried kissing happiness, it came very close to me and then pushed me away,' I said, looking at the glass of vodka in my hand.

'Wow Arjun! Which book did you pick this line from?' Krish said, putting down his bottle of Kingfisher beer.

'It's from the book of my life, titled *Loser*,' I answered nonchalantly and gulped down 60 ml vodka in one shot. My head spun for a moment, so did the world around me.

I put down my glass and looked at Krish. In that dim lighting of the open-roof Hint pub, I could see his round-neck T-shirt with a catchy slogan written on it – 'My brain is the second best organ of my body.' The quote brought a feeble smile on my face.

It had been two months since I left Hyderabad for Bangalore. Other than Anjali, Krish was my only good friend in this new city. In fact, he was the one who had brought me to the pub. Because he was bored of spending weekends with his nagging girlfriends. Yes, Krish was an irresistible flirt and girls drooled over him. Maybe it was because of his sense of humour, or his mesmerizing charisma. He had a long list of girlfriends and he could never find enough time for them.

'My dear strawberry, I am dying to speak to you, but my phone's battery is dying too,' Krish said to his girlfriend number...seven, I guess.

'Okay jaanu. Love you,' I overheard the girl say.

'Love you too, sweetheart.' Krish disconnected the call without even listening to her.

'These girls ... I can't live with them and I can't live without them,' Krish said to me.

'You have so many girlfriends and you enjoy life a lot. Then why on earth did you choose to spend a Saturday evening with a boring guy like me?'

'Because ever since you've come to Bangalore, I've hardly seen you smile. You don't talk to anyone. You are lost in your own world. You come to office early and leave really late. You don't seem to be living life at all. You merely exist.'

I simply smiled in resignation – not knowing what to say.

'Sorry if I hurt you in any way. But I am intrigued.' He paused for a while and continued, his voice showing genuine concern, 'What's your problem, man? If you tell me, maybe I can help you out.'

I smiled weakly, again.

'You and your enigmatic smile! Let me guess your problem. Three guesses, okay?' Krish said.

'Okay.'

He said, 'Guess number 1 – Girl. Guess number 2 – Girl. Guess number 3 – Girl.'

I chuckled.

'So, a girl is your problem? Love story, haan?' he asked.

'NO,' I said emphatically.

'Then?'

'Love stories.'

'Well, well, well ... this is interesting. We have a lovesick Romeo sitting right in front of a Casanova.'

'Given the way I find solace in alcohol, the title Devdas would be more apt,' I said, downing another glass of vodka into my empty heart.

'Another good line,' Krish said appreciatively, but I remained silent and faked a smile.

'Now, tell me your story ... I mean stories,' Krish said.

'You really want me to tell you, *now*?'

'Of course! The best stories are told in bars by broken hearts.'

'Well, where do I begin?'

'Right from the moment you saw the first girl,' he said and poured another 30 ml of vodka in my glass. I drank it all and started narrating the story of my life.

Act – I
Hyderabad

Shraddha

I studied at a tier-II engineering college in Hyderabad. It was the first semester of our second year of engineering. Rohan, Amit and I were sitting in the college canteen, eating samosas with chutney, watching girls, and rating their looks. Apparently, the criteria for rating were a girl's face, eyes, lips, hair, figure, breasts, dressing sense, walking style, attitude, and overall demeanour. What is a college without pretty girls?

3 Idiots – that's what our classmates called us. Yeah! We were kind of idiots, but not like the ones shown in that Aamir Khan starrer. We were more like those three guys in *Dil Chahta Hai*.

Amit was silent, thoughtful, and tender, like Akshay Khanna in the movie, except that he didn't possess any artistic skills. Rohan was flirty, mischievous, and sociable, like Aamir Khan, except that he was quite tall. And I was perennially confused in life and was always looking for that *one* special girl, like Saif Ali Khan, except that I wasn't so handsome.

Truth be told, I wasn't desperate or anything, since I'd always believed that good things happen to those who wait. So I let destiny decide the right time for my heart to be shot by stupid Cupid.

As the three of us sat in the canteen, Rohan pointed towards three girls who had just entered.

'Freshers for sure,' he said.

'How do you know?' I enquired.

'Look at their eyes filled with some unknown fear. And their body language is a dead giveaway,' he said and waved at one of the girls. Surprisingly, she came towards us, smiling, along with her friends. I was dumbstruck.

'How did you do that, fucker?' I asked in astonishment.

'I met her in the college bus this morning,' Rohan said, smiling mischievously. Amit joined him. And as usual, they made me look like a fool.

The girls wished us individually, 'Good morning, sir,' following the custom of juniors addressing seniors as sir.

Rohan asked them to take seats and began talking to them. The three girls sat facing him, just like sunflowers facing the sun.

After talking for a while, he asked one of the girls to sit beside him, the one he had waved to. Needless to say, she was the prettiest of the three. I had to switch places with her, which left me sandwiched between the other two girls. Amit began speaking to the girl on his right and I had no other option but to talk to the one who was left.

'What's your name?' I asked her casually.

'Shraddha, sir,' she said, her voice barely reaching my ears.

'Don't be so intimidated. I am not going to rag you or anything. Chill!' I said.

'Thanks, sir.' The pitch was slightly higher this time.

'So, how do you find the college? It's been some two weeks since your classes started.'

'It's amazing, sir. I am totally in love with the campus. And I am really looking forward to enjoying the next four years of my life in this college,' she said, excitement replacing the fear in her tone.

'That's good to hear. What was your CET rank?'

'127, sir.'

Damn! Getting a 127 rank out of one lakh students who had appeared for CET was no joke. My rank was somewhere near 1000.

'Great! You must be very proud of yourself.'

'Not really, sir. I expected a rank below 100.'

Girls, I tell you, are never really happy with their marks and ranks. The majority of guys would celebrate when they get just passing marks, but girls tend to dwell in sadness and create a puddle of tears even if they score 80 out of 100.

'Hmm, 127 isn't that bad. You seem to be quite talented,' I said, looking into her eyes.

She blushed and lowered her head. I began observing her. She wore a light pink churidar with a dupatta that covered her breasts fully. The matching earrings complemented her dress, but her hair tied in a plait gave her a conservative look. Her complexion was neither fair nor dark. Overall, looks-wise, she was average – the kind of girl you wouldn't really notice in a group of girls. Rating: 5/10.

She looked up after a while and our eyes met. I felt that she was expecting me to ask her a few more questions. I wasn't really interested, yet I asked her other formal introductory questions. Even though I was talking to her for the sake of it, she answered all the questions enthusiastically. Typical fresher, I thought.

Despite being her senior, I spoke to her more like a friend. And since she was staying away from her parents, as a good senior, I suggested that she gets herself a cellphone.

In case you found the suggestion absurd, cell phones were still uncommon those days. If you had a Nokia 6600, it was equivalent to possessing the latest version of an Apple iPhone.

She said she would pay heed to my advice and get a phone soon. Just then, Amit tapped the table to get everybody's attention. He looked at both Rohan and me and said, 'We have a Java class now and we are already short of attendance. Let's go or we will be asked to get out of the class even before we enter.'

It wasn't a joke, but the girls giggled. Rohan joined them, but Amit didn't bother to. We got up and left for the class, leaving the three girls behind. As we walked out of the canteen, I turned back and saw Shraddha watching me intently. She was smiling. She waved at me and said bye. I involuntarily waved back.

Rohan, Amit and I rushed to the class, but the professor was already there.

'You're always late.' He threw a disgusted look at us and the girls in the front row giggled.

'Come in,' he said and we quietly went to the last bench. Rohan started playing the legendary snake game on his phone while Amit got engrossed in reading a philosophical novel. I pretended to listen to the lecture, lost in thoughts of my non-existent dream girl.

■

I saw Shraddha again after three days in K-block as I was running through the corridors, rushing to a lab. As soon as she saw me, she smiled and said, 'Hii!'

I smiled in return and said a terse hi.

At that moment, I understood a simple communication funda, that the difference between a 'hii' and a 'hi' is more than just an 'i'. While the former showed enthusiasm, the latter showed formality.

I was already late, so I didn't stop to speak to her. The senior guy is showing attitude, she must have felt.

Over the next two weeks, our paths crossed about four times and every time there was nothing more than a pleasant hi between us. When we met for the fifth time, I was sitting on a bench near the college bus stop waiting for the bus. She walked towards me. She was wearing a peacock-blue churidar with a net chunni. God! For the first time I noticed her breasts. They were full, round, and firm. Rating: 8 out of 10. Damn! It was very difficult to look at her eyes as she was walking towards me. I hoped she hadn't noticed my stealthy glances.

'Hello, sir, you seem to be very busy these days,' she said, offering me a Dairy Milk chocolate.

I took the chocolate from her hesitatingly and said, 'Well, we have our internal exams in a few days. So ...'

'Oh.'

'So, how's it going? Made any good friends?'

'Yeah! Quite a few actually.'

'Nice,' I said.

After that I didn't know what to say and remained silent. Man! I totally sucked at small talk. Had Rohan been in my place, he would have had a full-fledged conversation by now.

'Can I sit here?' she said, breaking the silence and pointing towards the bench.

'Sure,' I said, moving a bit to make space for her.

She sat beside me and began talking. Since college was new to her, every little thing about it excited her. After a while, she asked, 'Sir, as a senior, if there is one free advice that you want to give me, what would it be?'

'Ma'am, my only advice to you would be to never ask a senior like me for any advice,' I said, mocking her tone.

She chuckled and said, 'Sir, I am serious.'

'Well, in that case, I'd give you three pointers, not one.'

'Please do.'

'One, your knowledge of subjects and your grades are never going to be proportional. Study textbooks and gain knowledge, but when it comes to exams, just refer to guides to score well. Two, no matter how much you study, do participate in extracurricular activities. Three, pamper your seniors as much as you can and be friendly with them,' I said, ending with a tinge of sarcasm in my tone.

'Achha! But is it necessary to maintain a good relationship with every senior, or is one good relationship with just one good senior enough?' Her tone was deliberately innocent, with very subtle sarcasm. I bit my lower lip and wagged a finger at her, feigning disbelief over her mocking me. She smiled innocently.

We talked a little more, continuing the conversation even after boarding the bus. In the end, before leaving, she asked me if I could get her my old textbooks as she was unable to find the suggested editions of the prescribed ones.

I said, 'Okay, will give them to you tomorrow in the canteen. Meet me at 1.30 p.m.'

'Sure sir,' she said, nodding her head, looking very cute.

The next day, I put the old books in a bag and took them to college. I waited for Shraddha in the canteen but she didn't turn up. I didn't see her at the bus stop in the evening either. So I had to carry the bag back to my room like a donkey carrying a load of clothes.

She met me the next day and said, 'Sorry sir, I was stuck in a lab experiment yesterday. The teacher wouldn't allow me to leave until I finished it. I am so sorry.'

'Well ... it's okay,' I said, pulling a notebook from her hand that she was using as a shield against her breasts. I wrote down my number on the last page and said, 'I will bring the books tomorrow again. In case we don't find each other, just give me a call from any of your friends' phones. Okay?'

'Okay sir,' she nodded.

But to my dismay she didn't turn up the next day either. I was pissed. I felt I was being lenient and she was taking me for granted.

She met me the next day as I was busy copying an assignment that had to be submitted in an hour. Before I could say anything, she began chanting her mantra of 'sorry'. She said she would definitely take the books on Monday. I went back to writing the assignment and told her this delay could have been avoided if she had a phone.

'Sir, how about I wait for you at the bus stop in the evening? We'll go together.'

'Will see ...'

And in the evening when I went to the bus stop, she was there, sitting on a bench swinging her legs. She saw me and stood up. A smile flashed on her face automatically. She had left her hair open and was looking much nicer. I don't know if I was getting used to her or she was becoming prettier. She looked beautiful that day. Thanks to that stupid assignment, I hadn't noticed anything when I saw her in the morning.

We sat near the bus stop and our conversation began. We boarded the bus and she went on and on.

After about twenty minutes into our chat, I felt a vibration. I checked my Nokia 1180, but there weren't any missed calls or messages. So I put it back. After a minute, I again, felt something vibrating. I checked my phone again but in vain. I thought it to be some kind of syndrome where you feel your phone vibrating even when it isn't. But it happened the third time and I was like 'WTF?'

Immediately, I turned towards Shraddha. She wasn't acting normal. Her eyes were hiding something and I saw her hand covering the tiny front pocket of her bag. It didn't take me long to understand.

I said to her, 'Well, Miss Shraddha, you lied to me, which is quite understandable given that I am a senior and you don't know me well enough. But I want you to confess now.'

'What, sir?' she asked. Her tone clearly indicated fear and lack of confidence.

'Think and let me know. I guess you know what I am talking about,' I said coolly.

'I don't get you sir,' she said, trying to sound confident, her expression clearly belying her words.

I asked her to give me her bag. She did so reluctantly. I tapped the little pocket of her bag and found the culprit. I had guessed right. She was already using a phone, but had lied to me about it. I felt extremely bad. It didn't make any sense for me to sit next to her. I asked the driver to slow down and got off the running bus.

I took a city bus to reach home, all the while thinking about how I had been made a fool. *Bakra*, a better word, I guess, and that too at the hands of a junior. Fuck! This world isn't the place for nice guys.

When I reached my flat, I realized my roomies were going for a movie and had booked a ticket for me too without asking me. The movie was good, but in some corner of my mind, I was still thinking about Shraddha. *How could she lie to me? Do I look like one of those guys who stalk a girl after taking her phone number? Couldn't she have confessed when I asked her in the bus?*

That night I wondered why I was so angry with her. After thinking for a while I got the answer – she had broken my *trust*. The foundation of any relationship. But her one lie had ruined everything.

■

The next day, I saw her standing outside my classroom just before the lunch break. When I came out, she tried to talk to me, but I ignored her and walked away. Two days later, she came to me while I was reading a book in the library. I left the book midway and scurried out. She came to meet me again while I was having lunch in the canteen a couple of days after that – I stopped eating and stormed out. As I was walking away, I heard her pleading, but I had firmly decided not to talk to her and it didn't matter how she felt.

I decided to travel to my hometown to take a break. Some stupid movie was being played in the bus and I was watching it just to kill time. I received a call. No prizes for guessing who it was. As soon as

I answered it, she started apologizing and explaining why she had lied. I responded curtly and she began sobbing.

Now this was absurd. What can a guy do if a girl starts crying other than become soft and pacify her? A woman's tears can melt even the strongest of hearts and I couldn't be rude to her anymore. But at the same time, I didn't want to be lenient. Inspired by a scene from the movie, I asked her to write down the word 'sorry' a thousand times.

■

When I came back to college, she met me at the bus stop in the evening. Her face was devoid of any expression. She handed me a folded piece of paper which had 'Sorry (1000 times) :P' written on it.

'Is this a stupid joke?' I asked annoyed.

She was trying to stifle her laughter and said, 'No sir. Please unfold it.'

On opening it I found that she had indeed written the word sorry a thousand times. I couldn't help but appreciate her neat handwriting. The thousandth one was as legible as the first.

'So, has the angry young man calmed down now?' she asked, trying to be nice without sounding sarcastic.

'Well ...' I said and looked at her.

'I've never apologized so many times in my life. Sorry once again,' she said, holding her ears and making a puppy face.

Seeing her expressions, I couldn't help but smile.

'Thank God, you smiled,' she said and let out a huge sigh of relief. 'You have no idea how tense I was for the past one week,' she confessed.

After that incident, Shraddha and I became close friends. We started meeting every evening at the bus stop and travelled together. We'd talk about anything and everything, which continued over chats even after we reached home. Each day, I waited for the evening to meet her again. The best part of all this was that we never ran out of things to talk about and our conversations would flow effortlessly. Time passed and we grew comfortable with each other. We loved spending time together. Life was good.

One day, I was watching a cricket match being played between my class and the mechanical engineering team. Amit and Rohan were playing while I sat alone on a bench outside the boundary. I heard a voice from behind and turned around to see Shraddha.

'Hello sir! Aren't you playing the match?' she asked, sitting down beside me. Earlier she would have asked for my permission before sitting.

'I wish I *could*,' I said wistfully.

She sensed something was wrong and said, 'Sir, are you okay?'

I didn't reply and she put her hand on my shoulder gently.

Well, that's the thing with girls. Once they become a little close to you, they observe your every action and, strangely, they understand what you are going through, without you speaking about it.

I remained silent.

'You can share it with me if something is bothering you.'

'Well, it's a long story. Some other time,' I said, watching the match as Rohan and Amit high-fived after taking a wicket.

'You can tell me now. You know I've bunked my class for the first time,' she said proudly, smiling. I smiled at her in return.

'I've been observing you, sir. Though you hang out with your friends and have fun, you seem kind of lost sometimes. Something must have happened,' she said.

Surprised, I looked at her. But as I was lost in thoughts, she observed my perplexity and said, 'When we share our pain with others, we feel better. I really want to know what happened. In fact, I want to know everything about you and...'

As she was saying something, I got a call. It was from Anjali, my childhood friend. We hadn't spoken to each other in years and it was a pleasant surprise to hear from her again after such a long time. We talked for a few minutes about school life and past memories. She disconnected the call saying she had to attend an anatomy class and would call me sometime again. I was happy for her. Her dream of studying medicine had come true.

As soon as I put the phone back in my pocket, Shraddha fired a question, 'Who is Anjali??'

'My school friend,' I said.

'Just a friend??' Shraddha said, stressing on the word just.

'Yeah.'

She let out a sigh of relief. I felt she was a bit jealous, but I didn't really understand why.

'So, sir, tell me – your problems, childhood, family, Anjali and anything that you want to. I am all yours ... I mean, I am all ears,' she said.

First tryst with sadness

I was about four years old and it was my first day at school. My dad used to work as a video journalist, and shot a video of me that day, right from the moment I woke up till I got into the school bus. Thanks to the video, the first day of my school remains quite vivid in my memory.

I was clutching my mom's pallu with one hand as we walked towards the bus stop, holding a lolly-pop in the other. A girl of my age was standing at the bus stop with her mommy. Her eyes were welling up with tears and she was hugging her mom's legs.

The girl was wearing our school uniform. Even though she was crying, she looked cute (I think only girls look adorable when they cry). She had puffy cheeks that were now red because of constantly wiping off tears, and round, black eyes. Her hair was parted in the middle and tied up with two navy-blue rubber bands.

The girl wouldn't stop crying, until after a while, when she threw a glance at me. Little did I know that she was actually looking at the lollypop in my hand.

I had just finished one and was about to pop in another one when I looked at her puppy face and instinctively gave the lollypop to her. I regretted it later, but thank the lord, she stopped crying.

Our moms began introducing themselves. I stood next to the girl, watching her as she happily ate the lollypop.

After a while she asked, 'What is your name?'

'Arjun.'

'I am Anjali,' she said.

She smiled and looked cuter. Soon, the bus came and we got in. We sat beside each other in the bus and waved goodbye to our moms.

Anjali and I sat on the last seat. She sat by the window, watching the world through it, holding my hand. As we reached the school, Anjali started crying again. I couldn't help but give her another lollypop from my bag, and she was cheerful again.

From that day onwards, for the next two years, Anjali would tag along with me everywhere – in the bus, class, during lunch, and while playing too. For the first few years I didn't have any problem, but as I grew up, I began making enough guy friends and I wanted to spend time with my gang. Somehow, having Anjali as a shadow became a huge inconvenience.

Though she had a few female friends in our class, she always had a problem with them. I was her only friend and, for some reason, she liked being with me. However, times changed and I began avoiding her slowly to spend more time with my guy friends. But the more I tried to avoid her, the more she clung to me.

In her efforts to get me back, she would try to entice me by giving me chocolates, gifting colourful light pens, finishing my homework, and offering me her lunch. I'd be nice to her for a day or two and then would go back to my old ways.

One day, she felt more ignored than usual and started crying. Even lollypops couldn't pacify her. I did my best to console her, but the more I tried, the more she cried.

I guess girls learn early in life that if they need a guy's attention and want to get things done, crying is the best way forward. Somehow, I feel they have a ready reserve of tears whenever the situation calls for them.

I wiped her tears for long that day and told her that we would strike a deal. In the bus, I'd be there with her, but in the class, we would sit separately in different rows. I'd still be near her, I promised.

To make her laugh, I told her she looked like a Barbie doll. And in an instant, a big smile flashed on her face, with tears still in her eyes. I had lied, but it didn't matter. With girls, it's all about saying the right thing at the right time. It doesn't really matter if it is the truth or a lie.

As time passed, Anjali and I drifted apart slowly. She did face some withdrawal pain, but got used to it eventually. She'd still do my homework sometimes and offer me treats too. I liked her and we gradually became best friends.

As I grew up, like millions of Indian kids, I began playing cricket. My love for the game was unparalleled. Many a time, I'd bunk school under the pretext of a stomach ache or fever to watch cricket matches that India played. For the ones that I'd miss, I'd make sure I watched the highlights.

Over a period of time, my love for cricket grew and after the sixth standard, it reached a high point. I used to dream about playing for the Indian cricket team someday – just like Sachin Tendulkar.

On my birthday that year, Anjali gifted me a Fenta cricket bat. (In fact, on every birthday, Anjali would gift me something or the other – handmade greeting cards, a keychain for my cycle key, toy cars, etc.)

Over time, I improved significantly at cricket and became the best player in my class that year. A guy named Siddharth joined my class that year. He was good-looking with a charming personality. He played very well too. He would hit boundaries and sixes like Virendra Sehwag and hog the limelight. I, on the other hand, was the captain of the team and toiled like Rahul Dravid. We got along well and together won many matches for our school. But I started hating him soon after Aditi joined our school.

Seventh standard classes had just begun. Our English teacher was explaining a poem written by Robert Frost but I was busy thinking about the match that we had to play the coming Sunday. I drew a circle on a paper and was setting the field virtually, by writing names of the team members within the circle. But then I heard a voice at the door, 'May I come in, ma'am?'

I raised my head and saw the most beautiful girl I had ever seen in my life. She was as fair as a fairy, with a lovely oval-shaped face and large hazel eyes. Her hair was slightly curly and reached just below her neck, a few strands falling on her forehead elegantly. Her smile was naturally endearing, and an out-of-place canine on the right made it more enchanting.

She wore the same school dress as everyone else. But somehow, even that dull school dress looked beautiful on her. The skirt was slightly above her knees and she wore ankle-length socks, which gave maximum exposure to her milky-white legs – a treat for the eyes. I had just entered teenage and had begun to get erections while watching hot heroines on TV. But with this girl, it was something different, some inexplicable feeling. She was my first crush!

As she entered the class, all the guys gazed at her, under the influence of teenage hormones. Girls were feeling jealous already and made faces. It was fun to watch Anjali as she had caught me watching this girl. Luckily for me, the new girl sat beside Anjali and Anjali began speaking to her pleasantly as if she had known her forever.

After the class I went to Anjali.

'Her name is Aditi,' she said, even before I could ask. 'Topper in previous school, rich dad's only daughter, and loaded with attitude,' she continued.

'Wow!'

Anjali gave me a disgusted look and walked away.

The next day, I saw Aditi near the playground with Siddharth and I felt pangs of jealousy in my heart. I was too young to really know anything about love and lust. But it felt bad when Sid and Aditi spoke to each other intimately. At that moment, for once, I wished I were Sid.

I never got much of a chance to speak to Aditi, even though I badly wanted to. God bless the science teacher who put Aditi and me in the same team to demonstrate an experiment at a science fair. She spoke casually with me and I loved every single minute of those two days I spent with her. But that was pretty much it!

The next year, thanks to my dedicated focus on cricket, I became a much better player. So much so that I was selected for the district under-16 team and I became a sort of a hero in school overnight.

Aditi met me the next day and congratulated me. She extended her hand to give a handshake and, when her hand touched mine, I felt butterflies in my stomach. It was the first time I'd experienced that feeling. Her palms were very soft and I wished I could hold her hand forever. But I had to let it go. She smiled and I almost died. She said bye, waving her hand, and I watched her hair bouncing a little as she walked away. God, she was extremely pretty.

Anjali saw all this from a distance, and came to me after Aditi left. She had brought me an original Team India cap. I took it from her and thanked her. I put it on, but thoughts of Aditi were still running inside my head. Silly as it may seem, it was one of the happiest days of my school life.

■

In a few days, the under-16 tournament began. I played well all through the tournament, but it was the semi-final match that changed my life once and forever.

It was the last ball and the opposite team needed to score two runs. The entire school was watching the game and everyone was tense. The bowler bowled on the leg side and the batsman flicked it towards fine leg. Everyone thought the ball would rush to the boundary, but I dived to my left and caught it. The entire school cheered as we won the match by just 1 run. I was ecstatic. All my team members rushed towards me and lifted me on their shoulders.

I was celebrating the moment, but felt some pain in my hand. In my excitement, I hadn't noticed that my wrist had been badly injured. I had to be taken to the hospital immediately. The orthopaedic looked at the X-ray and said that my wrist needed to be bandaged for a month and I won't be able to play the final. But what he said after that was devastating. He said that the wrist injury was complex and I'd be able to use my hand normally only after a year. And since frequent rotation of wrists would hurt and cause more damage, I wouldn't be able to play cricket, *ever.*

The earth under my feet crumbled and my heart broke into a million pieces. It was too hard to digest that I'd have to part ways with cricket forever. Cricket was my life and it was all I'd known since my childhood. If I didn't play it, I was as good as dead.

Sid was selected in the team in my place and he played well in the final match. Everyone lauded him for his performance.

Aditi never really spoke to me again and she became much closer to Sid. I felt like crap. Everyone deserted me, except Anjali. For some reason, she began taking extra care of me, spent more time with me and tried her best to make me normal again. Her presence was a respite in my otherwise gruesome life.

Time passed and my numbness continued. I'd cry for hours alone at night, but it barely helped the cause. I joined a boarding school the next year, away from everyone, and tried to start a new life. Anjali would write letters to me once every two weeks. I replied to her letters initially, but gave up eventually. Her family moved to another state and we lost touch with each other.

■

'Now, here I am, watching my friends play cricket as my junior is listening about my childhood trauma,' I said, looking at Shraddha.

She looked at me intently. I looked away from her to hide my tears, but a teardrop escaped from my eyes and began to roll down my cheek. It was so shameful to cry in front of a girl, and that too a junior. But emotions can't be controlled.

Shraddha put her hand on my shoulder and at that moment, involuntarily, I rested my head on her shoulder. She didn't fidget. She just let me be like that.

'Thanks. I haven't shared this with anyone in college before.'

'I am glad you did,' she said, genuinely meaning it. I just smiled, not knowing what to say.

We sat there for some more time and as she was about to leave, I said, in a somewhat stern voice, 'Shraddha ... don't you ever tell anyone that I cried, okay?'

'I am going to tell the whole world,' she joked and ran away.

'Oyee.'

■

A few days later, as I was walking from the canteen to my class, I saw Shraddha coming from the opposite direction, along with her friends. That day, particularly, she was looking quite stunning. I intercepted her and her friends left us alone.

'What's so special today?' I said.

'Today is my birthday,' she said.

Holy shit! I had totally forgotten about it.

'I am sorry,' I said. 'It's just that ...'

'That's okay,' she said, smiling.

I looked at her and said, 'You're looking very beautiful today.'

She blushed and her face was beaming.

'I am so happy. You've complimented me for the first time,' she said, smiling.

'Well ...'

'I have to go now. My friends will be waiting. See you in the evening,' she said, the smile lingering on her face.

I left for class then, but I couldn't concentrate at all. I felt bad for not remembering her birthday. Such an idiot I was! I wanted to make up for it.

When classes ended for the day, instead of taking the bus from college, I tagged along with Amit in his car. We went straight to an Archie's gift shop and bought a big teddy bear. He dropped me at Shraddha's hostel and left. She had been calling me frantically all the while and I didn't take her calls. She messaged me about ten times asking me where I was and why I was ignoring her calls, but I didn't respond. I instead waited for her at her hostel.

When she arrived at her hostel, she looked sad. I was hiding behind the teddy bear at the entrance. A small note was attached to it saying, 'Happy birthday Shraddha :)'

She saw it and her jaw dropped in surprise. She moved the head of the teddy immediately to see who was behind it. And lo! It was me. She was no longer sad, rather she was quite excited to see me with that cute teddy. She took it from me and held it close to her. She caressed its nose, made a baby face, and said, 'This is soooo cute. Thank you so much.'

I could never understand girls' obsession with chocolates, flowers, and teddy bears. All I knew was that they made girls happy. I chose a teddy over chocolates and flowers, simply because chocolates would be eaten and flowers would wither. The teddy would stay for quite a long time.

It felt good to see Shraddha so happy. She was a simple girl trying to find happiness in the little things of life. That night, we spoke on the phone for a very long time. She told me how her hostel mates kept teasing her by writing Arjun on the teddy bear's chest. I couldn't help but laugh at that.

As we were nearing the end of our conversation, her tone grew emotional.

'Sir, sometimes I miss my parents and feel lonely. But then, when I talk to you, I feel better. Thanks for being there for me,' she said softly.

I didn't say anything. She didn't say anything either. And neither of us disconnected the call. It was strange. We were just breathing into our phones. Silence was talking. After a while, I disconnected the phone thinking that she might have slept off. But she messaged me after like an hour. It read, '*I was feeling lonely for a while after the call, but now, I am lying on my bed, hugging the teddy tightly. And I don't feel lonely anymore. :)*'

I just replied, '*Happy birthday once again, Shraddha. Good night.*'

Our friendship became stronger with time and we were inseparable, until the day she called me and said that a guy had proposed to her.

The proposal

One day, Amit, Rohan, and I were doing an experiment in the digital communications lab and were talking to one another.

'So, when are you going to propose to her?' Amit said.

'Propose to whom?' I was baffled.

'Shraddha. Who else?' Amit said simply.

'What made you think that I love her? She is just a good friend. Nothing else,' I said honestly.

'Yeah! You look at the breasts of your friend,' Rohan teased.

'Fucker! How did you know?' I said.

'Rohan knows everything,' he said and raised his collar in self-appreciation.

'Well, it's true that I sometimes notice her breasts. But it doesn't mean that I love her. You don't fall in love with an entire person just because you love their boobs. Get it?' I said, making my point clear.

'So, you're sure that you don't love her?'

'Of course I am. I am just twenty years old now and I don't want to take such a big decision so early in life. You know that I want to love, fuck, and marry only *one* girl. I don't have any feelings for Shraddha,' I said.

'But she has feelings for you,' Amit said in a calm voice, as usual.

'How do you know?' I was confused.

Rohan answered, 'It ain't rocket science. Of all the people in college, she always chooses to spend time with *you*. She shares everything about her life with *you*. She looks admiringly and affectionately at *you*. She looks most alive in *your* presence. She lets you rest *your* head on her shoulder. She hugs the teddy bear that has *your* name written on it and ...'

'And ... *you* are all she talks about with me when you are not around,' Amit added.

'Well ...'

'As long as you're clear, it's fine. But knowingly or unknowingly, I feel you have ignited feelings in her. Don't do that, man! It's an unforgivable crime,' Amit said. Wise words from a wise man.

We finished the experiment and went to the canteen for lunch. After that, Rohan and Amit left to attend a seminar that I was not interested in. I sat on a bench behind the library and pondered over the conversation we had just had.

Over the next few days, I did observe Shraddha's behaviour objectively. It was obvious she had feelings for me, but since I didn't feel the same way, I continued being a good senior and a nice friend.

■

After a few weeks, one fine evening, she messaged me that she needed to talk about something important. I called her at night and she sounded tense.

'What happened?' I asked anxiously.

'Nothing,' she replied.

Girls can be weird sometimes. She herself had messaged me that she needed to talk and when I asked her what it was, she said 'nothing'. I learnt that as a thumb rule, when a girl says 'nothing', there is almost always something.

'Tell me what happened?'

'Hmm …It's that I met a guy recently at a friend's birthday party. He took my number that day and we began talking. But now he says that he loves me and has just proposed to me on the phone,' she said in a monotone.

'Hmm … that's cool. So, what have you decided?'

'I don't know. I am clueless. I thought I should ask you about it.'

'Well … If you like the guy, just start spending time with him. You'll get to know him better that way. And as time passes, you'll know automatically whether you love him,' I said, giving her all the *gyaan* I had on matters of love.

'Hmm …'

'Whatever your decision may be, just don't take it in haste. Give it some time …'

'Okay, sir, I'll do as you suggest,' she said.

We made small talk for some time and then said goodbye.

From the next day onwards, she kept telling me about the guy who had proposed to her. He indeed seemed like a nice guy who loved her truly and I felt he would keep her happy. A month later, she accepted his proposal.

I was happy for her. She'd found someone special in her life. But things changed from then. Little did I know then that life was never going to be the same again.

A few days after she said yes to that guy, the frequency of messages and calls between us decreased. We used to meet daily earlier, but gradually that too dwindled down to once or twice a week. I used to see her in college speaking on the phone to that guy and she looked quite happy. I began feeling a twinge of jealousy.

With time, the distance between us grew. She wouldn't message or call me at all, unless she needed something from me. Sometimes when I called her, my call would be on waiting and she wouldn't bother to even call back. Even in college, if and when we saw each other, she would just exchange a pleasant hi and nothing more. She would respond to my messages if I messaged her and pick up my phone if it rang, but it was nowhere like the way it had been before. There wasn't any enthusiasm or excitement. When I asked her what was going on in her life, she would go on talking about her boyfriend and, after a while, I'd feel like crap.

Eventually, I began missing her badly. She was all I thought about, day and night. I'd still hang out with my friends, but at the back of my mind, I'd still think how nice it would have been if I could share all the little things of my life with Shraddha. The affection that she had for me was waning slowly, and my feelings for her were growing considerably.

■

One fine day, I lay on the terrace, watching the stars and deliberating over what had actually happened to me. I realized that the problem was simple – it was that I had gotten used to Shraddha and I liked her immensely. Now that she wasn't being the same with me anymore, I was missing her badly.

No matter how hard I tried to explain to my heart to let it go and move on, it just wouldn't listen. All it wanted was the company of the good old Shraddha.

All night, I thought about her and about all the time I had spent with her. I wished I could relive them. As I kept thinking, it slowly dawned upon me that I had actually fallen in love with her. It was difficult for me to digest and understand, for my ego wasn't willing to accept that I was in love. But in my heart of hearts I knew that I loved her. It's just that I'd been oblivious to it.

Now that I had finally understood, I wondered what to do next. For once, I wished I could rewind time and propose to her on her birthday. But that wasn't possible. She had a boyfriend now and if I proposed to her, I feared I might lose even the little friendship that I shared with her. After thinking for quite some time, I decided that I'd lock all my feelings within my heart and throw the key away. I told myself that I had missed her in life and there was nothing that I could do about it now. The wise thing was to just let her go.

But then, it was insanely difficult to abide by my decision. Things grew worse day by day and I felt I was actually stuck in a catch-22 situation.

Shraddha began ignoring me slowly. I felt she was more than happy with her boyfriend and I didn't matter to her anymore. I felt bad but I chose to suffer in silence. Only Amit and Rohan knew of my predicament and they supported me emotionally, like best friends do.

The next two months were a living nightmare. I couldn't concentrate on anything, let alone my final exams. I stopped taking care of myself. I stopped going out and meeting friends. With long hair and a thick beard, I looked like Early Man, except that I didn't roam naked. I wasted almost all my time watching porn and playing video games. I stopped eating properly and grew thin. Most of the time, I wallowed in sadness, listening to sad Bollywood songs and relating to those painful lyrics.

After two months of inactivity, I went to college. The results of the second year first semester exams were out and I'd failed in two subjects. I'd been a topper in school and never scored less than 80 %. But now I had failed and it hurt. I hated myself for bringing myself into this situation.

Anjali, my best friend

One day, as I was playing Need for Speed, I got a call from Anjali. She had been calling me sporadically and I was speaking to her normally. She said she would like to meet me on my birthday. Even though I wasn't really interested, I couldn't say no to her.

On a Saturday morning, Anjali arrived in Hyderabad and asked me to meet her at the Eat Street restaurant. I got up lazily and looked at myself in the mirror. I looked quite ugly. So I went to a salon to get a haircut. The barber looked at me like I had just come from the Andamans. But he trimmed my beard patiently, cut my hair, and coaxed me into getting a facial. I gave in and he made me look much better.

I met Anjali in the evening, wearing a simple checked shirt, faded jeans, and canvas shoes. I wasn't very excited or anything. I was meeting her more out of obligation than interest. It wasn't that I had any problem with Anjali, but I was so immersed in thoughts of Shraddha that I had lost interest in everything else.

I sat there in the restaurant alongside the bank of the Hussain Sagar Lake waiting for her, thinking about the days in school that I had spent with Anjali. We hadn't seen each other in six years. I felt somewhat better as I was about to spend time with a good friend. She was one of the very few people who had always stood by me, no matter what.

She walked in about fifteen minutes later. I saw her and my eyes widened. She had become very beautiful and I wondered if it was the same Anjali that I knew in school. She still had those puffy cheeks and round black eyes, but they were complementing her beauty now.

She was wearing a white tee and pink pants. Her hair was loose, held by a pink hair band, which made them curl like a wave in the front. She was wearing some classy watch on her left hand and a pink bangle on her right. Needless to say the tiny pink earrings made her look prettier. She came towards me and said, 'Hiiiiii.'

I replied, 'Hi.'

'I hope I didn't make you wait too long,' she said apologetically. She hadn't let go of the habit of being extremely nice to me.

'Naah! That's okay,' I said.

'I've been waiting to meet you, Arjun. It's been so long since we've met. How's life and how are you doing?' she asked enthusiastically.

'I am fine,' I lied.

'By the way, here is your birthday gift,' she said, taking out a box from her purse. It looked attractive with a nice gift wrap and satin ribbon around it.

'Why did you ...' I stopped midway and looked at her.

'My pleasure,' she said and directed me with her eyes to open the gift.

I found a beautiful watch inside. My time was bad, but the watch was good.

'Thanks,' I said.

'You don't have to,' she said smiling.

'By the way, I brought something for you too,' I said.

'What?' She was curious.

I put my hand in my pocket, took out a lollypop slowly and gave it to her.

'You idiot,' she said and threw her handkerchief at me in mock anger. I acted as if it hurt. She laughed and I laughed with her.

Thanks to Anjali, I was smiling after a very long time.

That's the thing about school friends. Even if you meet them after years, you pick up where you left. The connection is instant.

We started talking about the good old school days. She had an amazing memory and remembered every single thing that had happened in school. I couldn't recollect even the major events. She went on talking and, as usual, I listened to her patiently.

Then, she held me by my hand and took me to the various food counters. I ordered a chicken burger with Coke and French fries. She took a fruit bowl and grape juice.

'I am putting on weight. I should reduce,' she said.

Girls and their obsession with weight loss are inseparable, I understood.

We sat with our food on a bench, enjoying the breeze alongside the lake, and began talking again. There was so much to catch up on. Anjali's insane ability to remember everything helped her remember all those weird names in botany and zoology, I guess. No wonder she'd been among the top 100 in the medical entrance examinations and joined a reputed medical college in Bangalore.

She asked me about my life and I promptly diverted the topic back to hers. She began talking about her anatomy classes, her hectic life as a medico, the ragging in college, and other things.

'So you aren't interested in any guy in your college?' I asked her.

'Noo,' she said, making an O with her lips.

'Why? Are you interested in women?' I teased her.

'Such an idiot you are!' she said and began laughing uncontrollably. Girls laugh a lot at silly jokes, no idea why.

'Then what? Don't tell me no guy has ever proposed to you. You do look good,' I said genuinely.

'Thank you,' she said and continued, 'Guys did propose to me, but most of them were despos and losers.' She sounded disgusted.

'Oh!'

'But there is one senior guy in college who is really sweet. His name is Rahul and he looks as cute as a younger version of Shah Rukh Khan. He is there for me all the time, helps me whenever I need something, and takes good care of me. He bears with my mood swings and tantrums, and still never gets irritated. He is like my *best friend* in college.'

I could imagine the plight of the guy, wondering how he must be feeling to be in proximity of a girl like Anjali and remaining just a friend. The way Anjali spoke about her senior, I did feel that she liked him. Maybe she was oblivious, just like I'd been with Shraddha.

'So what about you? Any girlfriends??' she said and winked.

'No.'

'You are interested in girls only, right?' she said and began laughing. She played the same joke on me that I had played on her.

'No, Anjali. I am interested only in guys,' I said intensely.

'Whaat! Don't tell me you are serious.' Now she was astonished.

'Yes.'

'Seriously??' Her face was losing colour.

'Calm down. I was just kidding,' I said and laughed.

There was silence for a few seconds and then a sigh from her. 'Phew! For a moment, you freaked me out,' she said. 'So, you haven't proposed to any girl?'

'Well ...' I shook my head looking downward and tried my best to control my tears.

Anjali became all sympathetic. She got up and sat by my side, put her hand on my shoulder, and asked, 'What happened, Arjun?'

'Disaster,' I said, trying to fight the lump in my throat. I was quite happy after a long time. But one simple thought about Shraddha was enough to break me down.

Anjali understood that it had something to do with a girl. She offered her handkerchief so that I could wipe my tears. I took it and sneezed hard into it. She didn't mind. I regained composure as people around us were watching me cry. It was embarrassing, to say the least.

After a while, Anjali prodded me to tell her what had happened and I narrated the whole story, right from the beginning till the end.

'She is unlucky to lose you,' Anjali said, trying to make me feel better. I didn't reply.

We sat in silence for some more time. I dropped Anjali to the airport later and we bade goodbye. She told me repeatedly to eat and sleep properly, and to take care of myself. I nodded my head like a school kid listening to his favourite teacher. The flight left, taking Anjali away with it, leaving me alone.

From the next day onwards, Anjali called me every single day, no matter how busy she was with her academics. Medicine wasn't like engineering where you could mug up one night and puke the next day and pass the exams. Medicos had to study a lot. I'd have abandoned education midway if I had been a medico.

She would call to ask if I had eaten my breakfast, lunch, and dinner on time. She would specifically SMS me before sleeping, to sleep early and not sit for long hours playing video games. She would implore me to go out with friends and have fun. I'd get irritated sometimes because of her over-concern, but most times, I'd feel better knowing that there was at least someone in this world, other than my parents, who cared about my well-being.

I'd call Anjali every time I felt sad and she would listen to me with all the patience in the world. Mostly, she would listen to me without offering any suggestions. But afterwards, whenever I was normal, she would tell me softly not to think of Shraddha and to move on in life. I'd listen to her, but would go back to my old ways again.

Third year, first semester exams were nearing and, as expected, I barely passed them. If it weren't for Anjali's prodding to study well, I'd have probably failed in all the exams. When I told Anjali of my exam results, she became furious. She scolded me for being a loser and said, 'Some stupid girl goes away from your life and you want to waste all your life thinking about her? How long will you stay like this? You're destroying yourself day by day and that too for a girl who doesn't even give a damn.'

What she had said was a hundred percent true. I felt like crap and hung my head in shame.

'Sorry,' she said after calming down. I remained silent.

'Arjun ... I can't see you wasting your life,' she said and continued, 'If you don't pay attention to your studies now and score less, you won't even be eligible to attend placements next year. I've seen a lot of people struggling to get a job after college. I don't want to see you in that state.'

I don't know what happened to me at that moment. Maybe it was Anjali, the fear of leaving college without a job, or I was fed up with the way I was living my life. I resolved at that very moment to stop wasting my time on Shraddha and start concentrating on my studies.

The very next day, I joined GATE coaching, not to pursue M.Tech after college, but to understand all the subjects of computer science engineering better. My life became pretty simple thereafter. I'd attend coaching classes in the morning, go to college, come back home and study till late at night. Porn CDs got replaced by textbooks and video games were replaced by educational videos. For four months, I immersed myself completely in studying, researching and learning. The best part about all this was that I was slowly forgetting Shraddha. I did miss her sometimes, but I'd soon push thoughts of her away and focus on studying well.

Anjali would call me every day and she was happier than me to see me doing well. Thanks to Anjali's prodding again, I even presented papers in IITs, with Amit and Rohan. It was a great learning experience and I didn't know at the moment that the events I attended were going to help me in the future.

I wrote the GATE and got a good rank. Before I could celebrate the success, fourth year first sem exams came around and, thanks to the coaching and intensive preparation, I topped the exams and my overall aggregate skyrocketed. Placements followed a month later and I cracked a job on day-0 itself. But the best part was that an American company based in Hyderabad, which was a dream company for many students, came to campus to recruit and I was the only one in class who was offered a job.

Thereafter, my life changed. People who'd called me an idiot now began calling me a genius. Those who had despised my company now started talking to me. Girls who would giggle whenever teachers scolded me began to show respect towards me. Even Shraddha came to me and congratulated me.

That day, I understood one thing about the world: for everyone, success matters more than anything else. Whether you are a good guy or not, no one really cares. All they really care about is how successful you are.

Though my outlook towards life changed from then onwards, the core of me remained the same. I valued Amit, Rohan, and Anjali, for they had always been the same, irrespective of my success or failure. I began loving my parents more and started speaking to them every day on the phone. For once, I was back to being normal and living life fully.

Neha

In the last semester of college, there wasn't much to study and so Amit, Rohan and I would just hang out in the college canteen most of the time. Our computer science department was planning to organize a technical fest and they needed organizers and volunteers. The three of us started attending their meetings only to kill time and get attendance in the name of the fest, if for nothing else. But as we involved ourselves in the discussions, we soon became part of the core committee. The experience of attending fests in IITs helped us a lot and we came up with many innovative ideas to make the fest interesting.

Amit took care of the finance committee, Rohan handled the hospitality committee, and I took over the organizing committee. Most of the headache was mine as I was the chief of the organizing committee that overlooked every other committee.

Rohan took many interviews in MTV Roadies style and finalized the volunteers from among juniors. People loved him and hated him at the same time. Amit dealt with finances like a CA. And I took care of all the background work, from selecting the events to assigning volunteers to each of them.

One day, as I was working on the logistics for the event, I heard a sweet voice from behind that was going to change my life forever. I turned to see a petite girl, wearing a pink short-sleeved T-shirt and blue denims. A shy Minnie Mouse cartoon was printed on the tee and the girl looked as shy as that Minnie Mouse. She had a small face with a straight nose, and shoulder-length, silky, straight hair.

'Sir, I'd like to be part of the tech fest,' she said.

'Contact Rohan. He is the one taking care of selecting volunteers,' I said.

'I spoke to him, but he is being quite arrogant, sir,' she said, wringing her hands. She looked extremely innocent at that moment and I couldn't bear to hurt her by saying no.

'I'll speak to Rohan and include your name. I hope I can count on you,' I said the last line just to sound strict. When people get something too easily, they don't value it.

'You can, sir. I will work hard. I promise,' she said, smiling. She looked cute.

'Fill in your details here. Name, year and section,' I said, pointing to a form and handing her a pen.

'Neha, 2nd year, Comp Sci,' she wrote and gave the pen back.

'Cool.'

'Thank you, sir.'

The next day, all the organizers and volunteers were called to the auditorium. Amit, Rohan and I took the stage. Rohan began talking about the events that would be held as part of the fest, the roles and responsibilities of individuals handling the events, budgeting, publicity, and everything related to the fest. Everyone listened to him with rapt attention.

After the presentation, the team of sixty was divided into three groups – one each under the three of us. And as luck would have it, Neha was in my team.

For the next one month, everyone was busy with something or the other related to the fest. Amit, Rohan and I took stock of the progress every evening. We planned things for a week in advance to ensure that everything went well. It was then only a matter of time for the fest to become a roaring success. Or at least that's what we thought. But how can a fest in an engineering college happen without any twists and last-moment panic?

Just a week before the event, the girl who was supposed to emcee the event fell sick. As I was worrying about it, Neha came to me.

'Sir, you look worried. Can I be of any help?' she said, with genuine concern.

'Nothing. I was just …' I stopped midway, suddenly struck by the idea that Neha could be made the anchor. She had a mesmerizing voice and an elegant demeanour.

'Are you interested in anchoring the event?' I asked, without preamble.

'Me, sir? I've never done it,' she said, fear writ large on her face.

'It doesn't really matter as long as you are confident,' I said, trying to infuse some confidence into her.

'I am not sure, sir. I am a bit scared.'

'Well … we shall do one thing then. Let's practise for some time in the evening. If it works out, well and good. Else, I will look for someone else,' I said.

'Okay sir, I will try. I will give my best.'

'See you in the evening at the auditorium. And don't call me sir. Arjun is fine.'

'Okay sir. Sorry. Okay Arjun,' she said, smiled, and walked away.

As agreed, we met in the evening. I had already prepared a sample speech.

First, I asked her to just read it and she did so fluently. Then, I asked her to modulate her tone in occasional crests and troughs. She did that well too. Then it was time to work on her body language. I asked her to put the paper on the podium and speak, with her hands moving freely in tandem with the speech. She couldn't do that well. So I held her hand and corrected her. It was a purely involuntary action. But it had some effect on her. For reasons unknown, she shuddered a bit. I didn't mind it in the beginning. But the hair on her forearms stood on end and I noticed goose bumps.

I withdrew my hand in an instant. We fell silent for a moment. I acted as if nothing had happened and began showing her the same gestures again, this time standing a little away from her.

I wasn't sure if she got her gestures wrong again deliberately, but after two more attempts, she said, 'Can you please hold my hand and show me once again? This time, I will do it correctly.'

I held her hand hesitantly and she was trying to stifle her smile by pursing her lips. The next time, she did it correctly. I appreciated her as we finished the entire sample speech.

Something was strange!

We met over the next few days as well for rehearsal and I must say that Neha surpassed my expectations. She would sometimes look at me intently while I demonstrated and sometimes affectionately while I instructed her. I didn't really mind as I was more focused on making the fest a success.

On D-day, I woke up early and was the first one to reach college. Amit and Rohan joined me after some time, followed by the rest of the organizers and volunteers. We took care of all the preparations to make sure nothing went wrong.

At around 10 a.m., students from various colleges began pouring in. Rohan and his team that managed hospitality got all of them registered and directed them towards the auditorium. The welcome event began soon.

I met Neha backstage, where she had gone with her friends to change into a sari. When I saw her, I couldn't help but notice how pretty she looked. She wore a cream sari with a pink border and a short-sleeved pink blouse with a *dori* at the back. She held the *pallu* of her sari with one hand, and the other hand had matching bangles. She looked perfect for the event.

She looked a bit nervous, so I motivated her to be confident. It worked, for she set the stage on fire and delivered a flawless performance. The welcome event went well.

During the day, except for minor hitches, everything went as planned. Neha rocked the valedictory event too.

After the event, everyone celebrated the success by dancing to groovy songs. I was content, if not excited. People knew I was the guy behind the event, but it was Neha and Rohan who hogged the limelight. Quite frankly, I was okay with that too.

After a while, I slipped away from the auditorium silently and sat on a bench near the library, reliving the last two days. I called Anjali and told her everything that had happened. As usual, she was very happy for me. After I disconnected the call, I saw Neha running towards me. She came to me panting, 'Arjun, where were you till now? I've been searching for you all the while.'

'Well ... it's just that ...'

'You know, today is one of the happiest days of my life. I don't remember the last time I was this happy. Everyone is complimenting me. Thank you so much for giving me this chance to emcee the event and for believing that I'd be able to do it,' she said, without stopping even for a second.

'You deserve it,' I said.

'I owe you a treat for this.'

'You don't have to ...'

'No, no. I insist. Are you coming to college tomorrow?' Fourth year students barely came to college after getting placed. She knew that perhaps.

'I am not sure,' I said.

'Okay, I'll give you a call tomorrow. Just let me know if you are coming.'

'Fine.'

'Okay Arjun. I need to go, my friends are waiting for me,' she said and started running towards the bus stop. But she came back after a minute.

'How will I call you? I don't even have your number,' she said, making a silly face. I gave her my number and she called me immediately.

'That's my number,' she said. 'Neha Junior', I saved it.

When I woke up the next morning, I saw a message. It read, '*Gud morning:)*'. No prizes for guessing, it was from Neha. I didn't reply. She messaged me again when I went for a shower.

'*R u coming to coll??? Surprise 4 u :)*' was the next message. I didn't reply again. She called me after some time and asked me the same question. I said I'd be coming.

She met me in the college canteen in the evening. No sooner had we met than she took out a blue-and-white striped T-shirt and said, 'Happy birthday, Arjun.'

I was surprised, to say the least. 'Who told you it's my birthday?'

'Rohan.'

'Oh well, but you didn't have to get a gift,' I said.

'It's just a token of gratitude. And guess what? I've become quite popular since yesterday. Already, four guys have proposed to me.' She giggled.

'That's fine. But I am sorry, I can't take it,' I said plainly.

'I will feel very bad if you don't take it. You have no idea how hard it was to select it,' she said, making a sad and innocent face.

I took the T-shirt reluctantly. Her face beamed in no time and I wondered how girls' moods change in an instant.

In an uncanny coincidence, Shraddha entered the cafeteria at the same time and saw me with Neha. I could easily see that she was jealous seeing me with Neha. Sadistic pleasure it was, but it felt good. I began speaking with Neha more affectionately, just to annoy Shraddha. It felt stupid, but who cares! She then left the canteen abruptly.

From that day onwards, things changed between Neha and me. She began to message and call me regularly. Initially, she would talk about academics-related issues. But soon, our talks drifted to silly day-to-day incidents of her life.

We didn't even know when we became close to each other. Daily messages and calls became a ritual and even a day without her call felt empty. I was slowly getting addicted to her. I loved listening to her sweet voice. It sounded especially sweeter when she called my name.

The first time we video chatted was late at night after her parents had slept. She showed me her room. It was very tidy, unlike mine. The bed sheets were neatly tucked under the mattress. All her clothes were properly organized in a wardrobe. Her nightdress was a plain cream-coloured tee and light-blue pyjamas that had stars and moon on it, like someone had hand-painted the sky on it.

That night, we spoke until dawn. She showed me all her childhood pics and narrated the story behind every single pic. She sent some to me, making me promise that I'd delete them soon after I saw them. I said yes, but which guy on earth deletes pictures of a girl?

I began opening up with her and started talking about my past, parents, friends, roomies, and every little thing related to my life. She was gradually becoming my solace. And without her knowledge, she was repairing my broken heart slowly, for I realized that a heart broken by a girl can be repaired by another girl only. We became inseparable with time and I started feeling something for her. We even began sharing non-veg jokes and it didn't dawn upon me until then that behind this innocent-looking girl, there could be someone naughty too. Even though she would say *'chhii'*, *'yakk'*, I knew she enjoyed every bit of the conversation. An innocent-looking girl with a naughty mind is a deadly combo!

Even though Neha dressed like a modern girl, she was quite conservative by nature. She'd never meet me outside college or come with me to restaurants or movies. We would only meet in the college. I was quite okay with it, for I did feel her presence with me all the time.

Our relationship moved to the next level when one day, while video chatting, she said that she wanted to show me the new dresses that she had bought. She went away for a while and came back wearing a short skirt with pleats. I was stunned. Her legs were super smooth and she looked extremely pretty.

'How am I looking?' she asked, holding the ends of the skirt with her hands, making an arc.

'Like a little angel,' I replied.

She disappeared again and came back wearing another dress. This time, it was a frock that was till her knees. This went on for some time and while she was changing, I began imagining how she would look nude. I felt a tingling in my pant, a hard-on. I think she figured it out from my expression. The last straw was when she wore a pair of extremely tiny denim shorts with a tight T-shirt. God! She looked sexy. She turned around and I realized then that her hips were a perfect 9 out of 10.

But she didn't wear it for long. Girls do this all the time, I understood later. They tease guys with a trailer, and just when the guy begins to enjoy it, hoping he would be able to see the movie, they pull the plug. Somehow, they derive a strange pleasure in making guys crave for them. I was learning.

After that incident, we became more open with each other. We would meet during lunch break in the canteen when Amit, Rohan and I were having lunch. She used to bring her friends along. I'd speak to Neha, and Rohan would handle the rest of the girls. For once, life seemed good and I was happy again.

Friendship and love

One day Amit and I were talking to each other in the college. Rohan was absent that day. Neha was also bunking to attend her cousin's marriage.

'So, are you going to repeat the same mistake again?' Amit asked.

'What mistake?' I asked curiously.

'By not proposing to Neha,' Amit said calmly.

Then I remembered the conversation I had had with Amit and Rohan in the second year of college, when they had asked me if I was going to propose to Shraddha. I had denied loving her and regretted later. Amit was talking about that mistake.

'Do you think Neha loves me?' I asked Amit.

'It's your job to find out. I do think she is attracted to you. But what's in her heart, only she will know,' Amit always spoke little, but those few words were always pearls of wisdom.

Later that night, I pondered over proposing to Neha. We had been talking to each other for about five months and understood each other well. I thought we made a great couple. But in spite of my gut feeling that she would accept my proposal, I wasn't completely sure. So I decided to test the waters.

That night, when Neha and I were having a video chat, I said, 'Neha, it's very difficult to imagine life without you.'

'Why imagine? I will be there with you forever,' she said and giggled.

I was relieved. But did that mean she loved me and wanted to share her life with me? Or was she saying that she would be with me forever as a friend? Given the type of stuff we spoke with each other, I didn't think she thought about me only as a friend. I was confused and back to square one.

The next day, I tried gauging her feelings in another way. I said, without being very serious, 'The day you get married I'd probably cry a river.'

Neha remained silent for a while and said, 'It wouldn't look good if the groom cried at his own wedding.' She laughed incessantly.

I was stunned. Now what did that mean? Wasn't she trying to say that she was fine with getting married to me? I laughed along with her and didn't discuss it further. But I felt that she was probably waiting for me to propose. I chose the day when everyone gets enough courage to express their love – February 14.

As the day was nearing, I tried my best to be in her good books. I'd make her laugh with my stupid jokes, listen to her long, silly talks and would take care of her in as many ways as I could just like a good boyfriend. I once told her about my plans to get married to a girl who would be my friend first and then my lover. She said that maybe such a girl exists in my life and I was probably oblivious. These subtle hints increased my faith in her accepting my proposal.

A day before Feb 14, I called her and said that I wanted to meet her the next day at any cost.

She chuckled and said, 'Anything special?'

'Of course, yes. But it's a surprise,' I said.

I wondered if it was really a surprise. Any girl would easily understand if a guy asks to meet her on Valentine's Day to tell her something important. I went to a jewellery shop in the evening to buy a ring, for I wanted the moment to last forever. I bought a heart-shaped gold ring with three tiny stones embedded inside the heart. I wasn't rich enough to buy her diamonds, but I already had a diamond inside my heart – Neha.

So I met her the next day in college, late in the evening, when everyone had left. I had asked to meet her in a coffee shop, but she reiterated that she didn't like meeting any guy outside as it might get her into trouble. I didn't really force her for I didn't want to spoil her mood.

So when she came to the cafeteria, I was tense. There was no one in the canteen except the staff.

We sat in a corner. She was telling me about her day, but I was least interested. As she was talking, I closed her lips with my hand. She was surprised.

I knelt down and took out the ring from my pocket, like they do in the movies. It had worked for all the actors. Girls would open their mouths in astonishment, shed a few tears of joy, and hug the hero. They would live happily ever after. I hoped the same would happen with me as well. As I was about to give her the ring, she did open her mouth wide in astonishment, but she didn't shed any tears or hug me.

She simply asked, 'What is this?'

'Neha, I love you and I want to spend the rest of my life with you.'

'But ...'

'But what?'

'But you are my best friend, Arjun.'

'What?'

'I like you, but I never thought of you in any other way. I didn't expect this from you.'

I was flabbergasted, to say the least. For once, my mind stopped working. One minute of complete silence followed. It took me that much time to understand what she meant.

'I hope you are kidding,' I said, not knowing what to say.

'I am not kidding, Arjun. Of all the people in this world, I thought you understood me and treated me like your best friend. But I was wrong.' Her face was serious.

I couldn't understand anything. Just a few moments ago, she was smiling. Now, she looked quite serious.

'But I do love you a lot, Neha, more than anything else. I can't imagine a life without you. You know that too. Don't you?'

'I don't, Arjun. This has come as a complete shock to me,' she said, turning her face away from me.

'So all these days you never understood that I had feelings for you? And you didn't have any feelings for me?'

'No. I treat you *just* like a friend,' she was almost shouting as she picked up her bag to walk away. I couldn't control myself.

'Friends??? You don't send rubbish non-veg jokes to your friend. You don't wear miniskirts and tight shorts for your friend,' I said angrily. My exasperation got the better of me.

'I never thought you would think this way, Arjun,' she said, paused for a while, and continued, 'I am really sorry if my behaviour ever made you think that I had feelings for you. I guess it's my mistake.'

She stormed out of the canteen while I watched her go.

I called Amit and narrated everything. He said girls are extremely unpredictable.

'So, what should I do now?'

'Persist or perish,' Amit said calmly, in his signature style.

'Explain.'

'Most girls say no in the beginning when you propose to them. It's their default answer. If you really want her in your life, you have to remain a good friend, be there for her all the time, and hope that she would someday change her mind. You have to *persist*.'

'Oh ... what about perishing?'

'Just walk away from her life. If you are really important to her, she will begin to miss you and make efforts to come back to you. She would at least try to speak to you in indirect ways. It's just that you don't waste time on her and move on with other things in life. If it's really meant to be, then it will happen anyway.'

'I am confused now. What do you suggest?'

'I'd say perish. The more you chase a girl, the more she will try to push you away from her. Let her miss you and realize your value in her life. If she doesn't come back, you will anyway know where you stand in her life.'

'Makes sense,' I said.

I disconnected the call, and began thinking what I should be doing now. What Amit had said made perfect sense, but I didn't really pay heed to his advice to perish. I was afraid that if I stopped talking to her, she would go away from my life permanently. I felt that I should remain her friend and change her slowly. I hoped that one day she would understand how much I loved her and she would love me back too. So I called her after some time. She answered.

'Neha, I am sorry if I hurt you, but I really love you so much.' My voice was dull.

'You have hurt me badly, Arjun,' she said.

'I just couldn't help but fall in love with you, Neha. It isn't just about how beautiful you are, it's that our wavelengths match too, right?'

She was silent and I continued, 'I have a good job in my hand. I can talk to your dad if you want. I am not that kind of guy who would make a girl fall in love with him and cheat her later. You know that, don't you?

'Neha, I am proposing to you for marriage, not just to be my girlfriend,' I said whatever came to my mind, directly from the heart.

'How can I explain to you, Arjun? I just don't have any feelings for you. You are my best friend. I *don't* love you.'

Now what can a guy say when a girl tells him that she doesn't love him? I said what seemed to be the most plausible thing to say, 'You don't have to tell me your final decision right now. Take your time and think over it. Even after that, if you feel the same, I won't bother you again.'

'I can understand that you love me, Arjun. But I don't want to lose you. I really like you as a friend.'

Now which guy on earth wants to be friends with the girl he loves deeply? It's like having chicken biryani right in front of your eyes and not being able to eat it. But then, I had no other option but to remain friends with her. So I agreed.

From the next day onwards, I tried to be normal with her, just like before. But she wasn't being the same. Many a time, she would throw attitude and talk to me like she was doing me a favour. I felt bad, but I persisted. Once you propose to a girl, everything changes, I realized.

Nothing improved between me and Neha. In fact, things went from bad to worse. Every time I brought up the topic of love, she would let out a sigh of discomfort and disconnect the phone. She was gradually losing interest in me. I felt that maybe she was expecting me to express the depth of my love. Simple messages and calls wouldn't help the cause, I felt.

So, one day I bought a bouquet of flowers for her. She threw them into the dustbin. I felt bad. But the same night, I sent her long messages about how much I loved her. She didn't even reply. I felt worse. I didn't give up though. Every day, I lived in the hope that someday she would understand and feel the same for me too. But I was wrong. I wasn't really *living* in hope; I was actually *dying*, little by little.

I tried to forget her, but I couldn't, not even for a moment, no matter how hard I tried. There were just too many questions running in my mind. Didn't she love me? If not, what was all that between her and me? Didn't she know that I was going to propose to her on Valentine's Day? Why did she ask me to be her friend when she wasn't behaving like a friend anymore? Too many questions without any answers.

In order to forget her, I slowly got addicted to drinking. As some wise man said, alcohol doesn't give you answers to questions, but it helps you forget the questions when you don't know the answers. It did help. I took to spending my nights sitting on a bench near the outskirts, drinking vodka. Late at night, when I came back home, I would write poems on love and sadness. Somehow I found solace in expressing my deepest emotions. In fact, I began enjoying writing and it was one thing that I looked forward to every day.

One fine day, I created an anonymous blog and posted all the poems I had written and shared them on Orkut too. Micro-blogging wasn't so popular then and people did read blogs. My blog became a hit in no time as many people could relate to the emotions I was going through. I started posting on the blog every week.

My other solace was talking to Anjali. I felt bad for ignoring her after Neha entered my life. When I called Anjali, she didn't ignore me. In fact, she was happy that I had called her after a long time. But in a matter of seconds, she understood that something was wrong in my life. I tried to hide my feelings, but I broke into tears in no time. I told her everything about Neha. She didn't judge. She never did. She consoled me like a mother consoles her crying baby. I felt somewhat better. It's in tough moments of life that you realize who really matters!

As time passed, distance grew between Neha and me. Sadness in me grew too, proportionately. But after many alcohol bottles and quite a lot of love poems, some sense began prevailing in me. I realized that the more I thought about Neha, the worse I felt. I wasn't really going anywhere with this indulgence in alcohol and sadness. I decided to get out of this situation. The first step was to stop being her pseudo friend. It didn't take long to realize that being friendzoned is like standing near fire. You stand there to seek some warmth, but get burnt instead.

I decided that I'd stop speaking to Neha. It was going to be the toughest thing to do, but it was only going to help me in the long term. I did stop talking to her, but I was still sad deep within and wondered how beautiful life would have been if Neha had accepted my proposal. *All I wanted was to spend my life with the one I dearly loved. Was it too much to ask for?*

One day, Rohan and Amit were ecstatic; they had received approvals from US universities. They were to leave for the USA soon and so we planned for some shopping the next day. Around afternoon, Amit came to my house in his brand new car with tinted glasses. We started for Hyderabad Central shopping mall and got a call from Rohan midway. He said that he wouldn't be able to make it as there was some painting job going on in his house and there was no one to supervise the painters. Amit and I decided to cancel the plan and go for a movie instead. As Amit was driving towards the parking lot of Prasads IMAX theatre, he suddenly stopped midway.

'Why did you stop the car here?'

Amit didn't answer my question. Instead, he pointed a finger towards my left and asked me to look in that direction. My eyes widened in shock and the scene I saw broke my heart into a million pieces. I couldn't believe it. I rubbed my eyes just to be sure and as reality struck, it hurt immensely.

I saw Rohan and Neha together. He was pulling her cheeks and she was hitting his arm in mock anger. They seemed very comfortable in each other's company. As I was still reeling in shock, Neha took out a scarf from her bag and tied it around her face. She sat on Rohan's bike and hugged him from behind and they left.

Amit and I followed them, but I later realized that it was a bad idea. What I ended up seeing hurt me more than a thousand pins piercing my heart.

Rohan stopped the bike at his house. There wasn't any painting work being done. Moreover, the door was locked and it was evident that there was no one in the house.

Neha got down from his bike and held his hand, her fingers intertwined with his. As they walked towards the house, Rohan threw furtive glances around and opened the door. He pulled Neha inside and shut the door.

It doesn't take a genius to understand what Rohan and Neha would have done after entering the house. Just the thought of it made me uncomfortably numb.

Amit understood my situation. He started the car and took me to a coffee shop. He started talking to me, but I couldn't pay attention to him at all. Images of Neha and Rohan together were flashing in front of my eyes and I couldn't evade them.

When Neha and I were still talking, I had asked her many times if we could go to a movie or a restaurant on my bike. She had always refused. But she was doing the very same things with Rohan. Moreover, what hurt the most was that my best friend was courting the girl I dearly loved. You don't hit on your best friend's love interest; it's an unspoken rule of friendship.

So just like that, in one shot, I lost faith in both love and friendship. The truth was way too hard to digest.

Amit dropped me at my flat after his futile efforts to console me. He did say in the end to call him anytime if I needed him. It was a weekend and my roomies had left for their home towns. I just slumped on the bed and didn't realize when the pillow was soaked wet with my tears. Here I was, living in an illusion, about how sweet a girl Neha was and how good a friend Rohan was, but they were having an affair, right under my nose.

I tried to evade my thoughts, but couldn't. I imagined them romancing and romping in bed, and I was disgusted. I lay there on the bed for a long time fighting my thoughts, eventually falling asleep. But when I woke up, I was starving. I went to the kitchen to find something to eat. There was an apple lying on the slab. I held it in my left hand and took a knife in my right to cut the apple. Then I did the unthinkable.

I slit my wrist!

The next day, I woke up in a hospital bed with Amit beside me. A syringe was inserted near my right elbow and blood was being infused from a bottle placed above my head.

After an hour or so, Anjali came rushing, anxiety written all over her face. She saw me and then spoke to Amit. He took her aside, but I don't know what he said. She then spoke to the doctors and nurses, introducing herself as a medico. They explained my condition to her and said that I was safe. She heaved a sigh of relief and came to me.

I couldn't look her in the eye. I felt ashamed. She put her hand on my forehead and ran her fingers through my hair.

'Everything is going to be okay,' she said, assuring me.

As I came to my senses, slowly, I began to realize the stupidity of the act that I had committed. I didn't really know what had happened to me. As someone truly said, people don't commit suicide to kill themselves. They commit suicide to kill the pain. I had done the same impulsively.

As I was lost in my thoughts, Anjali took out a book from her bag and began reading. She had rushed from Bangalore to Hyderabad after Amit's call. She had exams in a week, but still, for her, I was more important.

For the next two days, she was there by my side day and night, taking care of me. On the day of discharge, she burst into tears, hit me on my chest with her fist and said repeatedly, 'Why did you do this?'

I didn't know what to say. I didn't know I was such a coward. I felt like crap!

Anjali regained her composure after a while. She held my chin with her hand, lifted my head a little and said, 'Listen! If you ever, ever, ever need anything, I am always a call away. Okay? Just pick up that bloody phone and call me, okay?'

'Okay,' I said feebly.

Why did she like me so much?

■

When I came back to my room, my roomies welcomed me. They chided me and then teased me playfully. I was glad that they didn't shower me with sympathy. But after that incident, a part of me changed forever.

Over the next month, I was busy preparing for the final exams. Anjali would call me every day to never let me feel alone. I didn't know at the time that she had asked my roomies to stay with me all the time. Amit would also drop in every once in a while.

I spoke to my parents frequently and began visiting my hometown more often.

Neha, just like my parents, didn't know about the suicide attempt. She did call me once in a while and I spoke to her normally. I understood that she called me just to check if I was still pining for her. I didn't show any signs of that. So she understood by the end of the month that I wasn't really interested in talking to her anymore. Rohan called me too, but every time he asked to meet up, I'd make some excuse.

Neha and Rohan changed my perspective on love and friendship forever. I lost trust in the word 'trust'. Moreover, I hated how they pretended nothing was going on between them. If I hadn't seen them together, I'd have probably never known. I slowly understood why every time Rohan didn't come to college, Neha would be absent too. I had learnt a lesson: I should be more careful with people and shouldn't trust anyone blindly.

The offer

I was still to overcome the grief. But thanks to the support of my parents, Anjali, Amit, and my roomies, I managed to write my final exams well. I had a month before I joined the company that had offered me a job. I needed something to do meanwhile to kill time. So I began writing poems and blog posts again, in English and Telugu. They were simple, yet loaded with emotion, talking about love, friendship, and life.

After about a month, I received a mail from a man praising my poems. He said that he was a lyricist who had written songs for many Telugu movies and wanted to meet me. *Why would a famous lyricist want to meet me?* I was surprised.

He gave me his address and I went to meet him, out of curiosity, if nothing else. His house was a multi-storeyed wonder.

'Tea or coffee?' he said, as soon as I'd made myself comfortable.

'Thank you, but I don't drink either,' I said, being formal.

'So you only like drinking vodka,' he said and smiled. He had read all my blog posts, I realized.

I smiled and said that I did so only occasionally. And he came to the point after some small talk.

'I see that you portray emotions well in simple words. I am growing old and my tired brain isn't working as well as it used to,' he said.

'Okay,' I said. *What did he want from me?*

'There is a new movie being produced by a famous film-maker. It's a teenage love story and I have been asked to write the lyrics for the songs and ...'He fidgeted in his seat and then said, 'I was wondering if you could write for me.'

Wait a minute! A famous lyricist was asking me to write songs for him! It took some time for it to sink in.

'I will pay you well. Don't worry. But you won't get the credit for it,' he said, avoiding eye contact. I didn't say anything.

'Think and let me know,' he said, pulling out his visiting card.

I took my leave, all the while thinking about the offer. For once, I wondered if all this was a joke. But it wasn't.

I called Anjali and spoke to her about it. She was ecstatic. But expressed her concern about his unethical behaviour. She also said that this might be the first step towards something big and it seemed a wise decision to grab the opportunity. So I called the lyricist and told him that I would accept his offer. And for the next one month, I was completely engrossed in writing lyrics.

As Anjali had told me, it helped me in moving on in life. I'd convince myself that it was for the better that I didn't get a girl like Neha. But sometimes, I'd still push away all logic and begin missing her.

You can never really forget the ones you love, even if you don't like them anymore. That's what was happening with me as well. But the best part was that I was moving on, although slowly and steadily.

∎

A month later, I joined the product-based company by which I had been selected. It was a big company with over one lakh employees worldwide. Joining a corporate soon after college was an altogether different experience. Until then, I used to hang out with people of my age who belonged to more or less the same background as mine. My view of the world was limited. But once I started working, I befriended people from various cities, backgrounds, and age groups. There was so much to learn and so many new things to discover. I realized how I had lived a life of a frog in the well all the while. I was determined to work hard and make a name for myself.

At the same time, my bonding with the lyricist grew strong and he asked me to write songs for another movie as well. I loved it.

My daily schedule for the next six months was set. I'd wake up and go to the office enthusiastically, finish my work, and come back home. In the evening, I'd spend time talking to Anjali, Amit, or my parents. At night, I gave my hundred percent to writing beautiful songs. Office work kept me busy on weekdays, but on weekends, I'd just enjoy watching good movies and listening to melodious songs.

Life fell into a routine and I was feeling better. Even though I wasn't brimming with happiness, I was quite content. But then, life has strange ways of twisting a contented life. Call it fate or destiny, my life was going to change again, thanks to a simple call made by Amit on one not-so-fine day. Life would have been different if he hadn't made that call.

Yeah, life is a bitch!

Saakshi

On that fateful day, Amit called me from the US, asking for a small favour. His school friend was to come to Hyderabad to join a new company. She was from Vizag and since she didn't know anyone in Hyderabad, Amit wanted me to help her out with food, accommodation, and other things till she got comfortable with the new city. I agreed without thinking twice, simply because Amit had asked.

On Saturday morning, when I was still asleep, I got a call from Amit's friend. I told her that I would pick her up from the Secunderabad railway station and hung up. I got ready in no time and called her after I reached the station.

'Hi, where are you?' I said.

'I am waiting near the bookstall at platform no. 1,' she said.

'I am exactly near the ...' I turned and saw a girl with luggage near the bookstall. Our eyes met. She had large, fish-shaped eyes and her eyebrows were neatly trimmed. Though they were as dark as a moonless night, they shone very bright. She was dressed in a mustard kameez and a Patiala salwar which suited her well.

'Hi! Saakshi?'

'Ya. Arjun?' she said and smiled.

Her smile was beautiful, and a tiny dimple flashed on her right cheek. I didn't know why, but I felt like kissing that dimple. I couldn't for obvious reasons. Instant attraction!

Ever since Neha had left, I'd never really liked any other girl. It had been eight months since I stopped talking to her. I'd usually look at girls in my office and near my flat and appreciate beauty, like every other guy does. But I never really felt the spark and the connection which I felt as soon as I saw Saakshi. That's the magic of attraction I guess. You don't really know why the hell you like one person and dislike another. There's no logic to it.

'I hope I didn't make you wait for long,' I said, trying to emerge from the spell of her captivating beauty.

'That's okay.' She continued smiling.

I took the suitcase from her and she carried the airbag along with her handbag as we strolled out of the station. We got into an auto and headed to Madhapur, which had a good number of paying guest accommodation. We selected a PG that served good food and had basic amenities.

We met again in the evening to have dinner together. I took her to one of the several restaurants that served delicious Hyderabadi food.

'So, what do you want to order?' I asked her as she was browsing the menu.

'Hmm,' she said, and after looking at the menu for about ten minutes, she gave up and said, 'You order for me too. I always find it quite difficult to choose for myself.'

It sounded silly and I chuckled. 'You've come to Hyderabad for the first time. You should try the biryani. It's the most popular dish here,' I said.

'Sure, I would love to have it,' she said and I ordered chicken biryani.

She started talking about Vizag and its beautiful beaches, followed by her college, friends, and family. I wasn't really paying attention to what she was saying. I was completely focused on her eyes. I was so lost in them that sometimes her voice went mute. This had never happened in my life before.

'So have you ever been to Vizag?' she asked me. I took me a second to regain my senses and answer her question.

'Nope,' I said simply.

'You should come sometime. Maybe for my wedding,' she said.

Her last words hit me like a thunderbolt. Here I was dreaming about her eyes and she was talking about her marriage. I picked up the glass of water to calm myself down.

'Marriage? So soon?' I said.

'Not right away. But it's on the cards, as soon as my mom finds me a suitable groom. Given her requirements, she might easily take a year though,' she said.

I felt some sense of relief.

'What about your dad? Isn't he interested in getting a good son-in-law?'

'He left my mom and me when I was in class twelve. My parents are divorced,' she said. I stopped eating.

'I am sorry,' I said. I was shocked, to say the least. I saw her eyes were moist. We sat silently, eating our food, and didn't speak much after that. I should have said something to cheer her up. But I didn't really know what to at that time.

She paid the bill in spite of my protests. And we then headed for her PG. On the way, I told her that my roomie worked in the same company as hers. I gave her his number and said that she could contact him for any help in the office.

When we reached her PG, I said, 'You can call me anytime you need anything. Don't hesitate, okay?'

'Okay,' she said.

'You look good even when sad. But you look extremely beautiful when you smile.' I don't really know why I said those words; maybe I thought it would make her feel better. Girls love compliments, this much I knew.

'Thanks,' she said with a broad smile. That dimple flashed again and I guess, like a hopeless idiot, I fell in love, once again.

Over the next week, she called me sporadically every time she needed some information. And every single time, I picked up the call, no matter what, and told her everything she needed to know.

On Friday evening, before I left office, she asked me if I could meet her. I didn't think even for a second and said yes. We went to a coffee shop nearby.

This time she was quite cheerful. She began talking about her office, colleagues, the idiotic trainer who would not miss a chance to talk to her, stupid roommate, how she missed her mom sometimes, and her love for the city.

I dropped her to her PG after that. We decided to meet at 10 a.m. the next day as she wanted to see Hyderabad.

I went to her PG the next day at exactly 10 a.m. and waited near the gate.' Just five minutes,' she said when I called her. But she came out after twenty minutes, which was expected, given that girls usually take a lot of time to dress up. I was irritated but cooled down the moment I saw her.

She was wearing a lovely violet kurti and a white salwar. Her chunni had beautiful embroidery work on it. She was wearing matching studs and a gold chain was resting between her breasts. That tiny violet bindi on her forehead was the icing on the cake. She came towards me and said, 'Hi Arjun.'

I didn't reply. I was too lost admiring her beauty.

'Helloo,' she said, waving her hand in front of my eyes.

'You're looking very pretty,' I said. My voice sounded deep.

'I know that,' she said mockingly, raising an invisible collar. We left on my bike.

'Where are we going?'

'Surprise,' I said.

We travelled for about thirty minutes and reached the old city. I parked the bike a few metres away from the unique symbol of Hyderabad.

'Wow, Charminar!' she exclaimed. 'I've seen it on TV and online, but this is the first time I am seeing it for real.'

I loved that she loved the sight of Charminar. We bought tickets and went inside. She was as amazed as a five-year-old kid. After looking around inside, I took her to the shops nearby that sold jewellery without burning a hole in the pocket. She bought quite a few bangles and jhumkas, and looked ecstatic.

We then had a sumptuous lunch in a nearby restaurant which served various Hyderabadi delicacies, right from sira paya to biryani. After filling our tummies, we headed for PVR cinemas and watched a romcom movie. She was totally involved in it, but I took occasional naps in between. The lunch was perhaps too heavy for me.

In the evening, we strolled along the necklace road that ran along the Hussain Sagar Lake. We dined at Water Front and headed back home. While sitting on the bike, she put her hand on my shoulder for support. I felt a strange tingling sensation throughout my body.

When we reached her PG at around 9 p.m., she asked me if I could spend some more time with her. So we walked together from her hostel to the main road and back. All day long, we had been together and there wasn't even a single moment of boredom. I hadn't even realized how time flew.

Before going inside, she stopped and looked deep into my eyes. 'Thank you very much, Arjun. I felt so happy today,' she said, her expressive eyes meaning every single word.

'My pleasure, ma'am,' I said and smiled.

I went back home and felt happy after a very long time. The pain caused by Shraddha and Neha didn't bother me anymore. Just thinking about Saakshi brought a big smile on my face. I didn't realize how or when or why I fell in love with her. It felt like magic!

From the next day onwards, Saakshi would call me during office hours for no reason at all. My colleagues would understand from my expression that I was talking to some girl I really liked. Even after reaching home, Saakshi and I would continue talking on the phone about all the silly things that had happened during the day. We would meet regularly and spend hours together. There was a hub of restaurants near her PG, and it became our adda. We would sit there till late night and time would stand still every time I was with her.

Saakshi and I were slowly getting more and more comfortable with each other. Sometimes, I'd praise her and sometimes I'd mock her. She would hit me on my arm every time I teased her playfully and I'd do so again and again for her to hit me over and over again. God! I loved every single minute I spent with her.

■

On a Friday evening, she called me and asked if I was game for a movie. Why would I say no? So she booked the tickets and we went for the matinee show of *Ye Jawaani Hai Diwani* the next day. It was fun.

After the movie, Saakshi took me along for shopping. Her cousin's wedding was nearing and she bought a sari worth thirty thousand rupees for the occasion, which startled me a bit, as I felt that it was a bit too much.

As we came out of the sari shop, she showed me a necklace on her phone and said, 'How does this look?'

'Wow! It's so nice,' I said wide-eyed. I began imaging how beautiful she would look in a sari, wearing that necklace.

'How much does it cost?' I asked casually.

'Twenty-five lakh,' she said.

'WHAA! You are kidding, right?'

'No,' she said simply.

Soon we headed for her PG on my bike. I didn't say anything on the way. I mentally calculated the number of years it would take me to buy her such a necklace based on my current pay cheque. I was earning five lakhs a year. So, assuming that my salary would increase a bit after two years, it would easily take me about four years to buy her something like that. That's when I realized how rich she was. Filthy rich!

As I was doing the maths in my mind, she put her hand on my shoulder for support. And near a speed breaker, when I slowed down the bike, she brushed her soft breasts on my back. It was the first time she had done that and I thought it had happened accidentally. But she repeated it twice. I got confused.

'So, you don't have any girlfriend?' she asked casually.

'No.'

'Hmm.'

'You never had any boyfriend?'

She laughed as soon as I asked that question and said, 'I can't even choose a food item from the menu. How do you think I could choose a life partner for myself? I'd let my mom find a groom for me.'

'So there isn't any chance of a love marriage?'

'No way. My family is very orthodox and they would never approve of it. There are slim chances, though if the boy is from the same caste and if his family is as rich as ours,' she said matter-of-factly.

'I see ...'

'So what are your plans for tomorrow?' she asked.

'I don't know. All my roomies have gone home for the weekend. I'll probably pass time watching some movie and writing lyrics.'

'So there isn't anyone in your room now?' She ignored the fact that I was a lyricist.

'No one.'

'Why don't you show me your flat once? You've never taken me to your place,' she pointed out.

'My room isn't something like Charminar. You wouldn't really miss anything by not seeing it. Moreover, it's very disorganized,' I said, thinking about how untidy my room was.

'No problem. I will organize it neatly.'

'Well ... Let's go to some restaurant and have dinner instead,' I said.

'Hmm. Okay,' she said and smiled.

I didn't really want her to see my room. Porn magazines lay on the floor. Unwashed dishes in the kitchen. Underwear hanging on the window. I didn't feel it was a sight she would like to see.

We discussed the movie while having dinner and I dropped her to her PG. Just before leaving, I don't know why, she ruffled my hair and said, 'You are a buddhu!'

Buddhu means dumb and I didn't understand why she said that, but I didn't really mind. I was quite okay with whatever she called me. As long as she spent time with me, I was good.

That night, I lay on the terrace and pondered over the prospects of me being with Saakshi. First, she was against love marriage. Second, she had said clearly that her mom would never approve of her marrying someone from another caste. Third, she came from a very affluent family. The disparities were obvious.

Slowly, it dawned on me that Saakshi was way out of my league. Marrying her and producing kids was a dream that would never really come true. I felt pangs of pain near my heart. Maybe I should take a chance and try to express my feelings to her, I thought. But then I recollected my horrible experiences with Shraddha and Neha. I didn't want to lose Saakshi too. It was still okay if she was in my life, even as a good friend, but I couldn't afford losing her.

After careful deliberation, I decided to keep all my feelings within my heart. It was inevitable that, someday, her mom would find a suitable rich guy for Saakshi and she would get married to him. Until then, I thought I'd spend as much time as possible with her and make sweet memories for a lifetime.

You can't get everything you want in life!

∎

With time, it became routine for us to go to the movies, restaurants and other places in Hyderabad. We loved each other's company. I was falling in love with her. Her lovely eyes and her pretty smile with that cute dimple drove me crazy. It was so difficult to be in my senses.

On a fateful Saturday evening, after watching a movie, we sat near the steps of the hub of restaurants. She began showing me her cousin's wedding pictures. As I held the phone in her hands, her fingers touched mine and I could sense that something was going to happen.

I raised my head and looked at her intently. She moved her eyebrows up and down asking what I was looking at. The expressions on my face were a dead giveaway and she understood that I was admiring her beauty. She smiled, and her dimple flashed; I couldn't hold my horses.

I bent forward and kissed that dimple. I don't know from where I got the courage to do that. But I did, and a second later, I realized my folly. She got up in an instant and looked around hurriedly. There was no one.

'Buddhu, I live nearby. What if someone had seen?' she shouted at me angrily and left for her PG. I followed her and tried to stop her by holding her hand.

'I am really sorry,' I said pleadingly.

'Get lost!' she said as she walked into the PG.

I didn't know what to do. I tried calling her, but she wouldn't answer the phone. I felt like crap and hated myself more than anything else. She didn't take my calls for two days. She wouldn't even reply to my long apologetic messages. And just like that, I realized that things had gone from heavenly to hellish, in a few seconds.

For one whole week, I was completely lost. All the moments that I had spent with Saakshi would flash in front of my eyes and I couldn't dodge them. I shouldn't have kissed her, I told myself more than a million times. I felt very bad when I realized that I'd just lost another person I loved.

A week later, on a Saturday evening, I got a call from her. I couldn't believe my eyes when I saw her name flashing on the screen. I was ecstatic and astonished at the same time. I answered the call and said hello, slowly. I thought she would shout at me. But to my surprise, she spoke casually. After a while she said, 'I am feeling hungry. Let's go for dinner together.'

'Now?'

'No, tomorrow evening?'

'What??'

'Now only, buddhu. I am waiting at my PG. Come quickly.'

She had called me. *She* wasn't angry at me. *She* didn't even say anything about the kiss. I quickly dressed and went to her PG; she was already waiting outside the gate.

'So late,' she said and got onto my bike. I remained silent. She led the conversation and I was just listening to her silently, nodding my head occasionally.

We sat in the restaurant and, like a ritual, I ordered food for both of us. I was actually waiting for her to bring up the topic of the kiss, but she didn't. I wondered if it was all a dream and if I had never really kissed her.

We went back to the PG and, on the way, she put her hand on my shoulder, like she always did. I felt that usual pleasure, but I didn't want to screw up my life again. We took the usual stroll after reaching her PG and I was happy that she had forgotten everything. She smiled pleasantly before leaving and said that I was one of the best guys she had ever met. I remained perplexed, not knowing what she meant. Girls can be very confusing, I tell you. Even God cannot understand them!

■

Another week passed by and the relationship between us went back to what it was before I kissed her. She did bring up the topic of the kiss twice, but I dodged that and quickly changed the topic.

That Friday, she booked tickets for a movie and, as usual, I went along with her. It was the love story of a couple in their early twenties. There were quite a few kissing scenes and I saw from the corner of my eye that Saakshi smiled and looked at me every time a kissing scene appeared on the screen. I just smiled weakly.

On our way back, she put her hand on my shoulder and began discussing the movie. She brought up the topic of the kiss again and I didn't reply. After a while, she shifted a little and her boobs were now brushing my back. What the fuck! Girls will never understand how a guy feels when those soft breasts touch his body. I was looking at her dimpled smile in the rear-view mirror as her breasts were caressing my back. For me, it was an exercise in double control.

'I just remembered that I need to book my train ticket tonight, but my laptop isn't working,' she said all of a sudden.

'Well, you can take mine and return it later,' I said.

'Wouldn't it be a problem for you?'

'That should be okay.'

'Let's do one thing. We'll go to your room now and I will book the tickets now itself,' she said.

'Ummm ...okay,' I mumbled.

I felt she would really hate me after seeing my disorganized room. So I parked my bike outside the gate and asked Saakshi to make herself comfortable in the lounge on the ground floor. I brought the laptop from upstairs and gave it to her. She sighed and said, 'You want me to sit here and book the tickets?'

'Ya, any problem?'

She sighed again and said, 'Ya, only one problem.'

'What?'

'You really are a buddhu,' she said and proceeded to book the tickets.

I never really understood why she called me by that name. I mean, I wasn't very smart or anything. But I wasn't that dumb either. I then dropped her to her PG and she didn't even say goodbye before leaving. I sent a goodnight message to her and there was no reply from her. Maybe she was tired, I consoled myself.

We met again after two days and she began telling me about a guy in her office who had become a very good friend of hers. She said that he was from my college and asked me if I knew him. I told her that I knew nothing about him. She asked me three times if I didn't really know him and I told her patiently that I had no clue about the guy. She didn't say anything about him thereafter. I felt relieved. Which guy on earth wants to listen to his love interest talking about some other guy?

Life was passing like a breeze and the days spent with Saakshi were turning out to be the best days of my life. I enjoyed spending time with her and never ever lost control, no matter how many times I saw Saakshi's cute dimple. I didn't want to upset her again, at any cost.

Being with Saakshi, I forgot everybody else. I rarely made calls to Amit or Anjali or my parents. I only talked to them when they called me and that too only for a short duration. Anjali did feel bad sometimes, but I made something up and I knew she'd understand. I told her about Saakshi and her only concern was that I shouldn't get hurt again, as she had seen me going through a similar phase before. But at that moment, I knew that with Saakshi, things would sail smoothly. I was already prepared to not let her know of my feelings for her. I had no expectations from her. I knew she would never be mine and so I just wanted to spend time with her until she got married. I was clear about that and enjoyed whatever time I got to spend with her. But then, just when you think everything is going good, that is when life screws you up!

The spark between Saakshi and me slowly began to wane. She wasn't as enthusiastic to meet me as she used to be. It was a classic case of déjà vu. The same had happened with Shraddha and Neha. But Saakshi went a step further.

Earlier, Saakshi used to ask me to take her out. She would book movie tickets and force me to go along with her. But then, things changed. Now whenever I asked her out, she would make some excuse or the other. Every time I called her, she began picking fights for no reason at all and would turn anything into an argument. No matter how hard I tried to retain my cool and dodge those arguments, she would make it a point to argue for the sake of arguing. I couldn't understand her strange behaviour. There came a point when I shuddered even at the thought of dialling her number.

I was confused beyond hell and didn't really know how to handle the situation. I tried to recall if I had done anything to make her react this way. But no matter how hard I tried, I never really understood why she had started behaving oddly all of a sudden.

I didn't call her for a week and there was no sign of messages or calls from her. With much difficulty, I decided to ask her why she was ignoring me. So, I picked up courage and called her. 'Hey Saakshi! Can I talk to you for a minute?' I said.

'What?'

'I just want to know why you have been ignoring me for the past few weeks.'

'Don't talk as if you know nothing.'

'Explain please.' I was perplexed.

'How could you forget that you kissed me without my consent?'

'God! It was a long time ago and I apologized so many times.'

'But I understand your intentions better. You have been sticking around me and waiting for another chance. But I am not that type. You should know this up front.'

I was totally stunned. It was true that I loved her, but I'd not even touched her hand after that fiasco. I had no such intentions either. I was more than happy just being in her company. If I really wanted her, I'd have proposed to her by now. I tried to explain this to her, but she didn't budge. It was a futile exercise.

In the end she harshly told me to never call her again; she wanted to stay away from guys like me who hang out with girls only to find a chance to kiss them. I couldn't bear to hear her words anymore and disconnected the call. It seemed strange to me. Why would she be normal for a month and then bring up this topic again?

I tried in vain to figure it out and then decided to just let her go. It was evident that she didn't need me in her life anymore. There was no point in clinging on to her. It was an unusually sad feeling and the pain slowly took over me. Alcohol became my solace again. And thanks to that lyricist who had called me at the same time asking me to write sad love songs, I resumed writing lyrics. I wondered how uncanny it was for him to ask me to write songs that matched the events in my life so accurately.

I went back to being numb – my favourite state of mind. Thoughts of Saakshi filled my mind and I tried hard to delete her memories, slowly but steadily, until the day my roomie who was Saakshi's colleague told me something that blew my mind completely.

'Arjun, I saw Saakshi today in the parking lot,' he said. His voice was a little tense.

'She is not talking to me anymore, man,' I said sadly.

'I saw her with a guy,' he blurted.

'Oh, might be a colleague,' I said.

'Yeah, but,' he said and showed me a pic in which Saakshi was with a guy in a compromising position. I couldn't believe my eyes.

He continued, 'I went to the lowest level of the parking lot in office to get a friend's car and I heard someone whispering. When I glanced around furtively, I saw Saakshi and the guy making out in a car. The windows were tinted and the car was parked in a corner that no one usually goes to.'

The guy in the picture was the same guy from my college about whom she had asked me. It was unbelievable. How could she do it? She had told me many times that she would never have a boyfriend and would marry a guy of her mom's choice. Moreover, the very reason she had stopped talking to me was because she felt I was the kind of guy who wanted to kiss her. But what was she doing here?

I couldn't take it anymore. I passed out for one whole minute. Sweat beads formed on my forehead and I felt a strange churning sensation in my stomach. My roomie brought a glass of water and splashed it on my face.

Instinctively, I wanted to pick up my phone and call her. But I realized that she wouldn't answer my call anyway. Moreover, I felt that it was her life and I had no right to ask her what she was doing with her colleague. *Can't believe that I am the fool again!*

■

For the entire day, I wondered how Saakshi could make out with that guy. And that too in a parking lot. It was unimaginable. I looked at the pic again and again, and tried to convince myself that it wasn't Saakshi in the pic. But you can fool your heart, not your brain. It *was* her.

As I was lost thinking about her, my mom called. She and Dad were in Hyderabad and they wanted to know when I could meet them.

'We are near Dilsukhnagar. Where are you?' my mom asked me. I hadn't met them in a long time.

'Mom, I've got some office work and won't be able to ...'

Even before I could finish the sentence, I heard a deafening noise and the call got disconnected. I tried calling back, but I couldn't reach her. I tried calling Dad, but even his mobile was switched off. I was worried sick.

I headed for Dilsukhnagar with my roomie. On the way, I got a message on my phone from a friend. It read – 'Bomb blasts in Dilsukhnagar, high alert in Hyderabad. Stay put in your homes.' I was near tears as I read that message. I prayed to god that I didn't believe in to keep Mom and Dad safe. My roomie drove faster and when we reached Dilsukhnagar, it was a horrible sight. Dead bodies lay on the road in pools of blood. Police had put barricades around to prevent people from going near the site.

I looked around frantically and found a body that looked like my mother. I ran towards her in spite of the police trying to stop me. My fears had come true. It was her. And beside her lay my dad. Both dead. I knelt down, covered my face with my hands, and cried hoarsely. The police tried to pull me up, albeit sympathetically. I didn't relent. I couldn't bear to see my parents lying motionless on the ground. It was the saddest moment of my entire life. I wept uncontrollably and went almost insane.

My roomie held me up as I wasn't even able to stand up properly. He took me aside with the help of the police and I sat on the footpath. The tears that flowed became one with the blood-stains. Anjali got to know of this news from my roomie and she started for Hyderabad immediately. I cried the whole night until my eyes went dry. My roomies consoled me and took care of me till Anjali arrived the next morning.

The dead bodies were handed over to me by the police. I lit the pyres the next day and watched my parents getting burned to ashes. Anjali consoled me and stayed in Hyderabad for a week. I didn't feel like eating anything. I couldn't sleep. I couldn't do anything at all. I remembered all the times I had ignored my mom and dad. I never really spent enough time with them. Most of the times, it was because of the girls I had fallen in love with who had never really cared about me. The regret was killing me now.

Sometimes, I'd just call on my mom's or dad's numbers even when I knew that they were gone. It was senseless; yet I had some stupid hope that some magic would happen and they would pick up the phone. I wanted to listen to their voices just one more time. I understood what it meant to lose your senses when you lose the people you love.

After a whole week of insufferable trauma, I began digesting the truth slowly. Anjali kept telling me that I needed to become strong and start a new life and make my parents proud by becoming something in life. Her words fell on deaf ears. Reluctantly, she left Hyderabad after instructing my roomies to take care of me.

I started going to the office again. I'd finish my work silently, come back home, cry, and sleep. Thanks to my stupid heart, I called up Saakshi to tell her about my parents' demise. She didn't pick up the phone. I called her again. There was no reply. I called her again. This time she answered and spoke even before I said anything.

'I am not interested in talking to you. Can't you understand? Why are you irritating me? Stop following me *like a dog*,' she shouted at me.

I remained silent for a few seconds and then hung up. 'Like a dog' – the phrase reverberated in my ears. The scar on my heart that had formed because of my parents' untimely death had begun to heal somewhat. Saakshi's words had reopened my wounds.

I got up from my desk, switched off my phone, and wept incessantly. I had never hurt anyone in my entire life. I walked out towards the nearby park to get some fresh air and peace. I just wanted to lead a normal life, being happy with people I loved. God, if at all he existed – why was he playing games with me? Did I really deserve all this sadness in my life? Why did he have to do this to me? Questions popped in my mind and I didn't have answers. I stayed in the park all night and slept on a bench, until a cop woke me up the next morning.

I went back to my room to find my roomies tense. Anjali had made many frantic calls to them and they were very worried about me. They were relieved to see me. I called Anjali soon after and she began shouting at me. She was sobbing and told me how she couldn't sleep even for a minute the whole night. It was understandable. But I didn't say anything, not even a sorry.

She spoke to me for a long time that night and suggested that I leave Hyderabad and shift to Bangalore. She said that a change of location would help me get over all this sooner. She was right in a way.

I put in my papers and requested my office to relieve me as soon as possible. Meanwhile, thanks to my work experience, it wasn't difficult to get an IT job in a new company in Bangalore. I bade goodbye to my loving roomies and to Hyderabad, hoping to begin a new life, not knowing what Bangalore had in store for me.

■

'Well, that was quite poignant,' Krish said, offering me a tissue.

I blew my nose into it and tried to control my tears. I looked around and there was no one except Krish and me. I wondered why the waiter hadn't asked us to leave as it was way past the closing time. Later, I came to know that Krish was friends with the owner of the pub and all the waiters knew him well. Who is he not friends with, I wondered.

'It's good that you shared everything with me. Your heart becomes lighter when you share your pain,' he said.

I was too lost to even respond.

'Come, I will drop you to your room,' Krish said. I tried to get up, but I stumbled. I guess I was drunk. Krish helped me up and took me downstairs. He made me lie on the backseat of his car. I dozed off, only to wake up in the morning in my bed. I didn't even remember how I was carried from the car to my room.

Act – II
Bangalore

Kaagaz

The bus ride out of Hyderabad was painful. We drove alongside the hub of restaurants where Saakshi and I used to hang out. After a few minutes, the bus reached Begumpet, where I had given Shraddha a teddy near her hostel, and then we went towards Prasads IMAX where I had come to know the *other* side of Neha. Memories of the time I had spent with them began flashing in front of my eyes. They had once been the most important people in my life and were very special. But now, they weren't even a part of my life.

As the bus crossed Dilsukhnagar, I thought of my parents. I couldn't get over the guilt that I had always taken them for granted. All their lives, they had done everything they could to keep me happy, as if their sole purpose of existence was to see that I never suffered at any moment in any way. I remembered the times I avoided their calls to talk to the girls. I remembered all the lies I told them to avoid meeting them. I remembered all the times I got irritated when my parents repeatedly told me to eat properly and sleep properly and to take care of my health. They never felt bad even if I didn't really care enough for them. Or maybe, they did, but didn't let me know, because they didn't want me to feel bad.

Millions of thoughts were crossing my mind and I wondered if I could ever get a chance, just one chance, to turn back time and undo everything that I had done wrong. I wanted to apologize to them once. But naah! It was impossible. I had lost them forever.

Why is it that we value people only after they are gone?

I was lost in regretful thoughts and I don't remember when I slipped into sleep. I woke up in the morning after the bus conductor repeatedly shook me. I was in Bangalore. I called Anjali and she was already waiting for me at the bus stop. She smiled when she saw me. Happiness was evident on her face.

I smiled feebly.

She drove me in her car amid hectic traffic. If there is one thing that you will hate about Bangalore, it's the damn traffic. Steering through occasional congestions, we eventually reached a colony called BTM Layout.

Anjali had already made arrangements for my stay in Bangalore by paying rent and everything else for a 1 BHK. I didn't know about it as I hadn't really planned anything.

We stopped at a two-storey house which had a lawn. There was a huge gate in the middle and a small one at the end that led to the first floor.

An old couple welcomed us as we entered the house. They looked warm and friendly, and invited us to the garden.

Uncle, Aunty, Anjali, and I sat in the lawn where we were served tea. Uncle and Aunty started telling us about their sons and daughters – all of them married and settled in the US. Their youngest granddaughter was the only one in their family who lived in India. She was doing her first year of engineering in some college on the outskirts of Bangalore.

After sometime, they handed us the keys to the flat. Anjali and I went inside the penthouse. Uncle and Aunty were quite liberal I felt, for most landlords in India make a big fuss if a girl so much as enters a guy's room.

As I entered the penthouse, I was surprised to see that everything inside was properly arranged. I had expected an empty room. There was a bed with a light blue bedspread on it, a study table with a chair, and a beanbag too. One of the walls was adorned with lovely paintings. The kitchen had a fridge and all the necessary utensils that a bachelor like me would need. Anjali had also spoken to a cook who would take care of the cooking for me.

My room in Hyderabad had been messy with no aesthetic appeal. But this one was quite elegant. Of course, it was because of Anjali. (I think girls are obsessed with beauty. They make this world beautiful, by being beautiful.)

After taking the clothes out of my suitcase and arranging them neatly in the cupboard, Anjali made some hot coffee. She took the beanbag as I sat on the bed. She knew I was sad, but instead of talking about all the bad things that had happened in my life, she tried her best to cheer me up with funny incidents from the world of medicos.

Anjali stayed with me till late in the evening and then went back to her hostel. I sat on the chair, placed my laptop on the study table, and began penning down poems.

What would my life have been without Anjali?

■

On Monday, I woke up early. It was my first day at the new company. Since it was a product-based company, there was no dress code. So I wore a plain white shirt and blue jeans and left for work.

In the office, I was welcomed by a handsome man in his early thirties. He was my manager, Sanjay. Fair complexion, sharp eyes, and a pleasant smile added to his cool demeanour.

He shook my hand warmly and took me into a small conference room. There he spoke to me about general things in life, such as my hometown and hobbies, and asked if I had a girlfriend. It was unusual as I had expected him to talk about the company, work culture, and my role and responsibilities.

'You will know about it soon anyway,' he said when I asked him about my work in his team.

He dialled an extension and asked someone to join us in the conference room.

Soon, a young guy with long hair and a sparse beard entered the room. He wore a black T-shirt that hugged his muscular body with blue jeans ripped at the knees. A band on his right hand and a Chrono watch on his left completed his look.

After giving him a once-over I wondered if he had mistakenly come to an IT company instead of a rock concert. He did look like a rockstar.

'Krish, this is Arjun, our new joinee,' Sanjay introduced us.

'Hi Arjun. Welcome to the team.' Krish greeted me with a firm handshake.

'Krish has been assigned as your *buddy* until you get familiar with the way we work. You can trouble him for anything,' Sanjay said to me.

'Anytime,' Krish replied.

Sanjay got a call on his phone. A cute eight-year-old girl's face flashed on the screen.

'Aarti, my daughter,' Sanjay said and left the room, instructing Krish to take care of me.

Krish took me to my desk, which was right next to his. My seat offered a good view from the window.

Just before lunch, Krish called all the team-mates and introduced me to them. They didn't look so excited to see me; I wasn't a pretty girl, after all.

For the next one month, I went very early to the office and left quite late. I spent all day by myself, sifting through the project-related documents on the laptop and occasionally talking to Krish if I needed anything. He helped me generously all the time. He invited me twice to join him for lunch in the cafeteria, but I declined politely. One day he forced me to go along with him. He tried his best to cheer me up, but I hardly said anything, nodding my head once in a while. I wasn't interested in talking to anyone.

After work, at night, I wrote poems for myself and lyrics for the lyricist. The songs were earning him a good name and even though he was quite unethical, he did pay me quite well as promised. I was content with it.

I called Anjali once in a while and we met twice in a restaurant for dinner. Even though she was extremely busy with her post-graduation, she always found time for me.

And then life fell into a routine.

One evening, Krish tapped me on my shoulder and asked me to follow him.

'Where?' I asked.

'Just come, man,' he said and grabbed my hand and pulled me from the chair.

I went along with him to another block of the building. He opened the door to a room and inside there were two guys and a girl.

'Golu, Chhotu, and Ruchika.' Krish pointed a finger at each of them as he introduced us.

'Guys, this is Arjun,' Krish said to them.

They all said hi in unison.

Golu, as he was nicknamed, was quite fat. He was sitting behind the drums, spinning the drumsticks in his exceptionally big hands. It looked as if a giant elephant was holding a tiny cricket bat.

Chhotu, on the other hand, was lean and short. He had a guitar bigger than him strapped on his shoulder.

It was the first time I was meeting Golu and Chhotu. But I knew Ruchika. We were on the same team and she too reported to Sanjay.

She was standing behind a keyboard, trying to tune the synthesizer. She wore a look of great concentration.

Ruchika wasn't so pretty, but she wasn't so bad either. If there was one thing about Ruchika that appealed to everyone, it was her hour-glass figure. She had long, sexy legs too. Later I learnt that most guys wanted their girlfriends to have Ruchika's figure. Needless to say, girls in the office envied her. But Ruchika never really seemed to care about all this. She was quite disciplined and would always finish her work quickly and leave office on time.

'Welcome to Kaagaz,' Krish said.

In Hindi, kaagaz means paper and it did sound like a cool name for a rock band. So, Krish was indeed a rockstar!

'We want our songs to leave an imprint on everyone's heart.' Krish strummed the guitar while explaining the rationale behind the name of the band.

It was both surprising and refreshing for me. As I sat on a stool, Krish, Ruchika, Golu, and Chhotu started playing the music. Krish was the lead guitarist-cum-singer of Kaagaz.

They began playing the song '*Every breath you take*' by a retro band called The Police. I knew about the song because Anjali had once asked me to listen to it.

'So you play only for fun or even participate in any events?' I asked after they were done with the song.

'We do play at events occasionally, but our focus right now is on winning the inter-corporate competition,' Ruchika said, adjusting the keyboard.

'What's that?' I asked.

'There will be a competition held at the end of the year among all the IT companies of Bangalore. One band from each company will participate in it. Last time, we stood second,' Ruchika said. She looked dejected.

'We played hit numbers, man. The audience went crazy but the judges awarded the first prize to the other band that played original numbers,' Krish said.

A brief silence ensued.

'1 ... 2 ... 3 ... 4 ...' Golu said and started playing the drums. Everyone else joined in and began playing another song, in near-perfect sync. Their coordination was laudable.

'Our band's new song – it's an original composition,' Krish said while playing the song and singing dummy lyrics.

'What's the song about?' I asked.

'About a guy's feelings when he is about to lose the girl he loves the most,' Krish replied.

'Oh ...'

I listened to the tune for a few minutes and told Krish that I would be back soon and rushed out of the room.

I got a tissue paper, scribbled a few lines on it on the fly, and handed it to Krish.

I thought you will forever be mine,
But now I understand you don't care a dime.
Is this some kind of obvious sign,
That you leaving me is only a matter of time.
* Interlude *
Now that you have decided to go away,
I am clueless as to what to say
But I just hope that some distant day,
In my loving arms you will forever stay.

The lines were written to match the tune they were playing.

'Wow! The lyrics are quite good,' Krish said. They began playing the tune again, but this time with my lyrics.

They spent about two more hours fine-tuning the music. Eventually, the song came out very well.

I was happy.

Golu, Chhotu, and Ruchika left after a while. Krish and I went to the cafeteria to have some food and then to the rooftop of the office building. We began talking, leaning against the railing and watching the traffic. It was late in the night and Bangalore looked even more appealing in the city lights.

I had always been selfish when it came to talking with Krish. I spoke to him only when I needed something and ignored him most of the time. But he didn't mind at all. I felt it was time to make up.

'So ... were you always passionate about music?' I asked Krish, initiating the conversation.

Krish chuckled. 'Not really. I started learning the guitar in school because I had a huge crush on my music teacher.'

'That's interesting.'

'Yeah, as time passed, I began playing on stage. People used to clap and girls used to cheer. Slowly, the guitar became a part of my identity. My interest in the guitar waned soon, but I continued playing to impress girls. And ...'

'And what?'

Krish took out a cigarette from his pocket and lit it. He took a puff, blew out the smoke, and said, 'And I stopped playing it from second year of college. Picked it up again only after college ended. Now, I play the guitar to escape from the pain of life.'

Well, that was quite surprising. I mean, Krish was the coolest and the most cheerful guy I had ever met in my life. He had killer looks and quite a lot of pretty girlfriends. His friend circle was quite enviable and he partied every weekend. He was rich enough to buy whatever he wanted. Everyone loved him immensely.

I couldn't understand what he meant by wanting to escape from the pain of life.

'What pain?' I asked, out of curiosity.

'Nothing. Do you smoke?'

'No, I don't.'

'Want to try once?' Krish offered me the cigarette he was smoking.

I took it reluctantly. I had never touched a cigarette, let alone smoked one. But there is a first time for everything. So I inhaled it out of curiosity.

One puff and I began coughing incessantly.

Krish patted my back and asked, 'Are you okay?' He tried to take the cigarette from me, but I didn't give it back.

I took another drag followed by a few more till I had finished it. I asked Krish for another cigarette and smoked that one too. I don't know why I did that. Maybe there is some insane pleasure in self-destruction and hitting rock bottom because once you reach there, you can only go up.

My eyes became slightly red afterwards and I started feeling high, the kind that non-smokers get when they smoke for the first time. I stood there silently watching Bangalore and its people.

After a few more minutes of silence, Krish looked at me and said, 'Tomorrow evening, we'll go to a bar. I will pick you up from your home.'

'Okay.'

'See you then.' He left.

■

The next day, we went to Hint, a bar in Bangalore. It's where Krish guessed my problem and I told him everything about my life – about Shraddha, Neha, and Saakshi and how fate had played with my life. He listened to me patiently as I spoke with a heavily drunk accent. He dropped me home safely and I don't remember much about what happened after that.

'It's good that you shared everything with me. Your life is about to change,' I vaguely remember Krish saying just before leaving.

And yeah! After that evening, my life did turn 180 degrees. It was never the same again.

Arjun to Arjun 2.0

The very next morning, Krish came banging on my door. I was fast asleep. So, with great difficulty, I woke up and opened the door, only to see him dressed in a tracksuit, holding another pair in his hands.

I yawned and invited him in, surprised at his untimely visit. He threw the tracksuit on my face and said, 'Wear it and get ready in ten minutes.'

'Where are we going?' I asked him in a sleepy voice.

'Just wear it, man. You'll know soon anyway.'

I was confused. The mere thought of going for a jog filled me with dread. I tried hard to make an excuse, but Krish stayed adamant.

I heaved a sigh of relief when he took me in his car. But it didn't last for long as he parked the car near a gym. We went inside and he introduced me to his friends. Soon after, he convinced me to try the beginner level exercises, even though I was hardly interested.

I felt sore after he dropped me back to my room and I slept till afternoon.

Over the next two weeks, the routine continued. Every single day, Krish would take me to the gym. I hated it. I behaved like a whining schoolboy who didn't want to go to school. But Krish was a taskmaster and he wouldn't relent.

He explained to me the anatomy of muscles and made me do exercises for the chest, lats, biceps, triceps, abs and legs, as per a schedule he had prepared. He also prepared a diet chart for me that had mostly protein-rich foods. I wondered why, since I was least interested.

By the end of the second week, Krish was making me do the bench press. I was exhausted and was ready to give up after ten repetitions, but he pushed me to do five more. I thought I wouldn't make it. But, I eventually did. A sense of achievement filled me, even though it wasn't really a big thing.

'Problems in your life are like the weights in the gym. You can either get weighed down by them or turn them to your advantage and become stronger,' Krish said.

It sounded philosophical, but it did make sense.

Afterwards, Krish and I went to Dosa Palace to have delicious chicken dosa. I was starving and as I was digging into it, Krish said, 'Which celebrity do you think most girls drool over?'

I thought for a few seconds and replied, 'Hrithik Roshan.'

'Why do you think so?'

'Because of his chiselled body, just like a Greek god.'

'Good. But do you think those same girls would love him if he had a potbelly?'

I understood why Krish wanted me to be physically fit. 'Looks don't matter is one of the greatest lies ever told. A muscular body is to a guy what a good figure is to a girl.'

I pondered over his statement for a while and it made sense. I never knew of a girl who wouldn't get attracted to a fit body. I didn't know at that moment that exercising would help me improve not only physically, but emotionally as well. I would become more disciplined in life; my willpower to do important things would increase. It also became a habit to push myself out of my comfort zone.

Once we were done with our breakfast, Krish took me to a hair salon. He whispered something to the hair dresser and they smiled. I sensed an experiment coming my way. All my life I had had a side parting and my hair was neatly combed. But that was going to change now.

Krish stood between me and the mirror all along, so I couldn't see a thing. When he moved aside, and couldn't believe the sight I saw in the mirror. The side-parted hair had given way to spiky hair. But I did look somewhat good, actually, much better than I had all my life.

In the evening, he took me to a dermatologist and signed me up for a treatment to remove tan, pimples, and blackheads. It did burn a hole in my pocket but Krish's logic was that there was no point in having money if you couldn't buy some happiness with it. 'Looking good and presentable makes one confident and happy,' he said.

The last task in improving my appearance was the shopping spree that lasted for a week. My wardrobe was filled with either checked or plain shirts, which were replaced with funky T-shirts and jeans.

Over a period of a month, the way I looked changed completely.

I met Anjali after that and she couldn't believe her eyes. 'Oh my God!' she exclaimed, when she saw me first. 'Someone is looking handsome.'

I didn't understand why, but Anjali was very happy that day. I realized later that when a girl likes a guy, any kind of improvement in the guy's life makes her immensely happy. Maybe she felt good to see me looking better than I ever had. Or maybe the looks had masked the pain that I hid inside!

Life gradually started becoming better, even though I did feel sad sometimes, especially during late nights when I'd sleep on the terrace watching the stars. I would miss my parents terribly.

But then, going to the gym daily, working hard in the office, grooming myself, writing lyrics – these things did keep me busy, helping me overcome my sadness.

I grew close to Golu, Chhotu, and Ruchika. We had lunch together and enjoyed cracking stupid jokes. We would comment on other girls in the office and, contrary to my expectation, Ruchika joined us too.

I loved Ruchika's street smart jokes and dark sense of humour. I didn't want to be outdone. So I too started cracking jokes. For some reason, Ruchika loved them and she would high-five me on most occasions. She would sometimes playfully tap my arm too when the jokes went a little off the board. She loved them anyway.

Golu and Chhotu's camaraderie was to die for. They would tease and crack jokes about each other's physical appearance. But what I loved most about them was that they liked each other immensely. Though Golu would put his arm tightly around Chhotu's neck every time he didn't have a good comeback, it was always laced with indulgence. And if anyone else made fun of Chhotu, Golu would be the first one to defend him.

I felt a sense of belonging as I was made the lyricist of the band. I was feeling content as I started writing new chapters in my life.

Anjali was quite happy too, simply because I was forgetting the past and moving on in life. I used to tell her everything – about Kaagaz, gym training, lyrics-writing sessions, office, friendship with Krish, and almost everything. No one else in the world knew me better than Anjali. She had always been there for me – every single time.

Life was finally moving on the right track, although slowly, until one Saturday when I had the longest conversation of my life with Krish. It was a once-in-a-lifetime conversation. And after that, my life moved into the fast lane.

The enlightenment

When you look back, most days in life seem ordinary, but there are some that change your life forever and remain etched in your memory.

One Saturday night, Krish and I went to our favourite pub. He was wearing a black tee and faded blue jeans. 'Sex is the consolation when you don't have love' was imprinted on his T-shirt. Where the hell does he get these T-shirts from, I wondered.

We sat on the same table where I had shared the story of my life with him. Krish ordered beer for himself and vodka for me, along with Sprite, chicken drumsticks, chilly chicken, fried kaju, and, most importantly, masala peanuts.

'So how's the song coming along?' Krish asked me, removing his wristband and placing it on the table.

'Which one?'

'The one on women and what they want.'

'Well ...' I sighed and said, 'Dude ... I can't for the life of me understand women. They are so confusing and complicated.'

Krish chuckled and I continued, 'I wish there were some formulae or algorithms to figure out women. You put some variables and you get the result. Wouldn't life have been simpler then? I would have escaped all the tragedy in my life.'

I couldn't help the engineer in me get the better of me, bringing up variables and equations in a discussion on women.

Krish laughed and just when he was about to say something, his phone rang. It was a girl. He disconnected it, leaned forward, and said in a profound voice, 'Women aren't as complicated as you think. Women, if not handled properly, can be your greatest cause of sorrow. But the same women, if dealt with deftly, can be your greatest source of pleasure.'

He then asked, 'Why do you think I brought you here today?'

'Why?'

He didn't answer my question, but looked at me and smiled. I guess I knew what he was up to. He wanted to tell me about girls and their psychology. Even I was curious to know coz there were a lot of questions in my mind to which I didn't have any answers.

'Before I tell you about girls, let's analyse your life, all the mistakes you committed with your girls and lessons to be learnt from them.'

'Let's do it.' I was game.

Meanwhile, the waiter brought our drinks. Krish opened a beer bottle for himself and poured some vodka for me.

We had a sip and began what I could say was the longest conversation of my life.

'So the first thing that you need to know about girls is that they never *directly* say what they really want or how they truly feel. They almost always use the indirect mode of communication.'

'Okay!'

'What was the first girl's name? I am sorry I forgot,' Krish said, rubbing his forehead with his fingers, trying to recollect the name.

'Shraddha,' pat came the reply from me.

'Ya Shraddha. So when Shraddha told you that she felt better when she hugged the teddy bear gifted by you, with your name written on it, what do you think she was trying to say?' Krish paused for effect and continued, 'All she was trying to say is that she wants to hug you and she feels better when she imagines hugging you.'

'Ohh.' I was silent, but my jaw dropped open in surprise.

'So you must always decode what a woman says versus what she really means. In fact, one of the greatest differences between nice guys and flirts is the latter's ability to decrypt.'

It made perfect sense now. I recalled Shraddha's voice when she had told me about hugging the teddy bear. It had been intense and full of love. I felt like an idiot for not understanding her emotions.

Krish read my mind again and said, 'Don't worry. Everybody makes mistakes. The greatest mistake one could make is not to learn from those mistakes.'

'What's the second thing about girls that I need to know?' I was intrigued.

'The next thing you should know is that at least in the initial days of a relationship, a girl doesn't really ask you how you feel about her or what you think about her. Instead, she judges you on how you act in different scenarios and forms an opinion about you,' Krish said, waving his hands like a professor while teaching his students.

'For example?'

'When Shraddha called you and told you about some guy who had proposed to her, why do you think she told you that?'

'Because she was clueless and she wanted guidance,' I said, without thinking much.

'Bullshit!' Krish replied. 'She was in love with you, man. All she was trying to do was check if you too loved her. But when you behaved like her gay friend and suggested she spends more time with the other guy to know him better, she concluded that you didn't love her. As simple as that.'

I was taken aback as I let his words sink in. Krish started munching on peanuts waiting for my reaction.

I picked up my glass and finished the entire 30 ml in one shot.

'I agree with you buddy, but if she really liked me, how do you explain her avoiding me soon after accepting the other guy's proposal? Couldn't she remain a friend? Her ignoring me like a piece of shit hurt me more than her rejection.' I became emotional while saying this.

Krish poured another 30 ml of vodka in my glass along with some Sprite and stirred it.

'For any girl in this world, in the beginning of a relationship, and especially when it's her first love, her boyfriend becomes the most important person in this world. She just can't help but think about him all the time. She gets involved with him so much that she ignores her friends, family, and everyone else. That's what happened in your case too.'

'You are taking her side, dude. Not fair.'

'I am not taking sides, man. I am just stating a fact. And from my experience, I can tell you that girls don't do this deliberately. They become obsessed with the guy they love. It's the way they are designed,' Krish said.

Now, I could somehow figure out Shraddha, but I still could not understand where things went wrong with Neha.

So I asked Krish, 'Okay … with Shraddha, it was my stupidity. But what about Neha? It's a big mystery to me till date. Everything was going well and I proposed to her only after testing the waters. She seemed to be interested as well. Why the hell did she reject me?'

'Because you proposed to her,' Krish said simply.

'Whaat!!?'

'Ya, she rejected you because you proposed to her.'

Maybe I was drunk or Krish was being cryptic for, I couldn't understand what he really meant. Saying she rejected me because I proposed to her was akin to saying a person died because he was born.

Frustrated, I took a piece of chilli chicken and stuffed it in my mouth. I lifted the glass of vodka and took a sip. Krish began to explain in a way I understood.

'Listen to me carefully. What I am going to say might seem very unconventional to you, because it's totally against the way a guy's brain is programmed by society.'

I put down my glass on the table and paid attention to him, even though I was slightly drunk.

'See, when you propose to a girl, you are actually allowing her to make a very conscious decision. In other words, you are allowing her brain, not her heart, to make a decision.'

'Hmm.'

'Her heart comes up with all the pros about you, but her brain comes up with all the cons. Her mind gets filled with millions of thoughts. But since our human mind always attaches more weight to cons than pros, her thinking gets clogged. She might end up thinking that she hadn't developed feelings fully or she might wonder if she would get a guy better than you, or she might begin thinking that a future with you isn't really feasible and, to be better safe than sorry, she rejects you even if she has some liking for you in some corner of her heart.'

'Achha.'

'Moreover, when a girl is getting to know you, you are an unsolved puzzle to her. She begins to wonder whether you like her or not. She tries to decode your actions and decipher meaning from your words. She becomes intrigued trying to figure you out and she enjoys this process. But once you confess your feelings honestly to her, the element of mystery is gone. You deprive her of the pleasure she used to get in figuring you out. And ... she no longer feels attracted to you.'

I used to think that Krish was a flirt and a philosopher rolled into one. But after listening to his analysis about women's minds, I wondered if he had done a course on women psychology too.

'My bladder is full of beer, man. Will be back in a moment.' Krish excused himself.

I was too lost in thought to even say okay. I began stirring the vodka and Sprite involuntarily as Krish's words stirred in my brain.

It was quite difficult for me to digest what Krish had said, but as I cross-checked his words with what had happened in my life, things did start making sense. I remembered how Neha had stopped showing interest soon after I had proposed to her.

Though I was almost convinced, a few questions still lingered in my mind.

Krish came back and took out a cigarette. He offered me one and held the lighter for me. We took a puff and our conversation resumed.

'Dude, I have a few questions in mind about Neha.'

'Go ahead.'

'If she didn't really love me, why did she have those video chatting sessions wearing skimpy clothes?'

'Because she felt like doing it.'

'So it doesn't amount to anything?'

'It does, man, but not so much. You need to know that women are more emotional than logical. Most decisions they take and most things they do are just based on their mood, emotions, and intuition.'

'I still don't get your point.' I was confused. All these revelations about women were too much for me to take.

'You see, if you begin to think that *because* she had some hot video chat with you she must be thinking of you as her future boyfriend, you are applying logic there. But using logic to understand women is like using emotions to understand computer programming. It just doesn't work.'

Now I understood what Krish was trying to say. I recollected how Neha's conversations with me were dependent on her moods.

Her tone, her choice of words and her actions – all reflected the emotions that she was going through at that moment. But I was still not completely convinced. It's so difficult to change your beliefs overnight.

I took a deep puff of the cigarette and said to Krish, still hoping to defend my assumptions, 'You remember, before I proposed to Neha, I told her that I would cry at her wedding and she said that it wouldn't look good if the groom himself cries?'

Krish chuckled and said, 'Yes.'

'Why do you think she said that?' I asked.

'You are again applying logic, man.'

'But she did say that, right?' It was my last-ditch attempt to justify my proposal to Neha.

'She also said that she would never meet you outside of college, never get on your bike, never go to any restaurant with you, and never to the movies. But she did the exact opposite with Rohan, right?' Krish said.

The mention of Rohan's name took me to the day I had seen him with Neha, which had eventually compelled me to attempt suicide. I looked at my wrist. The mark was still there.

'I am sorry to take you back to your painful memories. But I want you to get over all this, once and for all,' Krish said, genuinely meaning every single word.

'Yes, even I want to. So, what's the point you are trying to make when you say that Neha did exactly the opposite of what she had said to me?'

'It's that – you should never really apply logic to judge a girl and instead understand her emotions. Also I want to reinforce the point that most of the time, girls don't really mean what they say and don't really say what they mean. So you should always judge her by her actions and not her words.'

'A little more elaboration, please.'

'Well, I will give you a very common example. Suppose a guy asks a girl out but she gives him some lame excuse saying she has some work or the other. Most likely it means that she is avoiding him. The words that she blurts out while giving the excuse don't mean anything at all. Her reluctance to go out with him speaks volumes.'

Listening to Krish, I felt like I was a certified idiot. How could I not understand simple things like these for so long? Why did it take someone like Krish to make me realize these little nuggets of wisdom? I would be more circumspect now on, I decided.

Krish was watching me intently as I was brooding over his words. It's then that an important question popped up in my mind.

'So you say that I made a mistake by proposing to Neha. But then, proposing to a girl after she becomes closer is logically the next thing to do, right? What else should I have done?' I said.

'You should have kissed her.'

'Whaaaaat!!??'

I knew that Krish was a flirt and all, but sometimes he did get weird. He was saying that I should kiss a girl before proposing to her. It made no sense at all to me, at least at that moment.

'I know it may sound weird to you, but that's what you did with Saakshi, right?' Krish said, sipping his beer.

'Oh ... yeah.'

'So what happened next?'

'She did some drama initially, but then she became closer to me in the next few days,' I recollected.

'Exactly!'

Many a time in life, I guess we know the right thing to do. But most times, it takes someone else to tell us that. In my case, it was Krish.

I was silent for a few seconds and Krish continued, 'See, kissing a girl is a calculated risk. Most of the time, things do turn out in your favour.'

'Calculated risk?'

'Ya, when you kiss a girl, you leave her with only two options – either she should leave you forever or she should stay with you.'

'Achha.'

'If she leaves you forever, which most often doesn't happen, it's a clear indication that she isn't interested in you. You can then forget her and move on. But if she comes back to you, it means she herself is indirectly showing interest in you. Things will move further from that point automatically and she would most likely become involved with you, without you proposing to her at all.'

'Ohh.' I was silent for one whole minute. It took me that much time to understand the innocently cunning logic behind kissing a girl.

'So you say that I did the right thing by kissing Saakshi. Then what went wrong with her? Why did she leave me for some other guy?'

'Because you didn't proceed further. Simple.'

'Ohh ... but she didn't seem that kind of girl. She said she would never have a boyfriend,' I said.

'She didn't seem like that to you because you got lost in her words and didn't read between the lines.'

'I don't get you,' I said honestly.

'Why do you think she brushed her breasts occasionally when she sat pillion on your bike? Why do you think she asked you to take her to your room making some stupid excuse of booking train tickets, not once but twice? Why do you think she nicknamed you Buddhu?'

'Fuck!' I said astonished. Krish didn't have to tell me the answers.

'Couldn't she have waited for me? Maybe I would have known her true feelings after some more time,' I said, becoming impatient.

'She did wait long enough,' Krish said plainly.

'Hmm.'

'Moreover, there is something called "attraction window",' Krish said.

'Attraction window?'

'Yes. Attraction window is the time period during which a girl slowly begins showing interest in you and is getting attracted to you. It's usually in the initial days of her getting to know you and when she begins feeling comfortable with you.'

'Okay.'

'During this time, she is least inhibited by your advances and most receptive to them. This time is the proverbial good time of your life when anything you touch becomes gold. In fact, the girl gives enough hints to you to go physical with her.'

'So you mean to say that during this period a guy should kiss a girl and take things further.'

'Yup! But there's a twist here. If you proceed correctly, things will turn out hunky-dory and you can have lots of fun. But if you don't act within this time frame, the girl gets pissed off, will lose interest automatically and may leave you forever. After that it becomes almost impossible to turn things around. The same girl that would do anything to be with you will then do anything to avoid you. That's what happened with Saakshi,' Krish concluded.

Every single word that Krish had said was fucking true. I correlated his words with the events that happened in my life. I began to understand girls' behaviour better. It was like a revelation, like finally figuring out the mystery in a crime novel.

Krish snapped his fingers in front of my eyes as I was lost in thought. I regained my senses and said, 'Why do girls do that, dude? Why do they leave soon after the attraction window is over?'

'That's a mystery to me too, man. They leave maybe because their ego takes a beating or they feel they are wasting their time on you or they get dejected after a while. It's just a guess. But all I can say is – that's the way a woman's mind is designed and I think even she can't help it.'

Krish then went on to tell me the right things to do during the attraction window, like holding a girl's hand first to test the waters and then to kiss her fingers first. If she doesn't protest too much, it most likely means she wants the guy to proceed further. He then told me about making the girl comfortable first and choosing a place where she doesn't have to worry about privacy. And then, in a very carefully planned but seemingly unintentional manner, the guy should softly plant his lips on hers.

Krish understood women very well and knew exactly which buttons to push at what time. He knew how to give a girl heavenly pleasure. It slowly dawned on me why some girls prefer experienced guys to freshers.

I was memorizing every word spoken by him, especially about holding hands and kissing, but I had one more confusion to clear. 'Doesn't a woman hate it when a guy touches her? Wouldn't she build a negative opinion of him if he does that?' At least that's what I knew from my social conditioning.

He said, after tittering for a while, 'There was a girl in my life who once sat on my lap and complained about how she hated her boss touching her. I stroked her waist gently and said that maybe he found her too attractive to resist. She blushed and hugged me tight.'

'What's the point?' I asked.

'What I am trying to tell you is that a woman doesn't dislike being touched, but the kind of men who touch her. If you touch her heart properly, she will let you touch every part of her body.

'In fact, every single part of a woman's body craves for touch. However, if she doesn't like a guy, she will get upset even if he touches her fingernail. But if she likes a guy, then she would welcome his touch. And will get pissed if he doesn't touch her. Makes sense?'

'You, sir, are a genius! Thanks for the enlightenment!' I folded my hands in appreciation.

Krish raised his hand as if he were blessing me.

We both remained silent for a while.

I turned around to see where the sudden whistles and hoots were coming from and saw a pretty girl staring at the floor, her face expressionless. I looked down and saw a guy kneeling in front of her, holding something. He seemed like a gentleman, neatly dressed and quite classy. He held up a bouquet of roses, a teddy bear, and Belgian chocolates. I asked Krish to look at them and he began laughing, as if he knew what was going to happen.

The guy proposed to her with a diamond ring. It looked like a scene straight out of a Karan Johar movie. I thought the girl would accept his proposal. But to my surprise, she pulled her hand away from him unsettlingly and walked away annoyed. The guy was left stranded. It reminded me of the day I had proposed to Neha. I felt bad for the guy.

Krish was still laughing and I could not fathom why. He saw my face and stopped laughing, and asked me instead, 'Now explain to me – how does a guy who never showered love on a girl end up sleeping with her and how does a gentleman who makes her feel special by proposing to her get rejected?'

I was already confused and Krish's question just went over my head.

'Come, let's go,' Krish said, picking up the cigarette packet, and we left the pub after paying the bill. We picked up a crate of beer from a nearby wine shop and headed for BTM Layout. Krish steered his car towards a deserted lane and stopped near an abandoned park. We got out and sat on the pavement, beer bottles in our hands.

'Today, I am gonna tell you two very important things about how to get women. These two are primary and everything else is secondary. Just pay attention and listen to me very carefully,' Krish said. His tone grew intense.

I put down the bottler of beer.

'First, you should constantly strive to become awesome and make your overall life awesome.'

'Okay.'

'I believe that every guy has some special skill in him. I play the guitar and sing songs. Your talent lies in writing beautiful lyrics and it makes you awesome. So, the first thing you need to do is identify your talent and strive to become the very best in it.'

'Okay, but how does it help get girls?'

'When your overall life becomes awesome, you become attractive automatically. You begin to exude confidence and girls will start liking you subconsciously. You don't need to do anything to impress them.'

'I get your point,' I said.

'The second thing is that just being awesome won't suffice,' Krish said, breaking my train of thought.

'Then?'

'You should also mingle with a lot of people and try to expand your social circle as much as you can. There is no point in being awesome and living in the Himalayas. No girl would even know of your existence then.'

'Achha.'

'So it boils down to a very simple equation. The number of women you end up having in your life is proportional to your awesomeness and the number of women you meet or get to know.'

Being an engineer, I was quite happy that Krish had boiled down the dating success to an equation. It also explained Krish's success with many girls. Krish was not only an amazing person, he also had extremely good socializing skills.

Thinking more about the equation, my belief in Krish's words was reinforced, as he had shared his own experiences with me and not some stuff written in psychology books. I wondered how many years it would have taken him to understand these intricate details.

As I was busy thinking, Krish decided to take a stroll.

So we walked along a narrow path with cobblestones, enjoying our beer. Krish began, 'I can go on talking about women, but before we call it a night, I want to tell you one last thing about women.'

'Okay.'

'Again, this goes against conventional thinking. So just stay with me till the end.'

'You know I will,' I said.

'What does the mother board of a laptop or a cellphone look like to the naked eye?' Krish asked.

'Why do you ask me that?' I was confused.

'You'll know soon anyway. First answer my question,' he said and smiled.

'Well ...,' I said, trying to recollect the electronics topics I had studied in my engineering. 'To the naked eye, a motherboard looks like a series of complex, interconnected circuits through which the current flows.'

'Exactly!!' Krish said. I was still confused and couldn't see where he was trying to head to.

He continued, 'You see, a woman's brain is like that complex circuit and the emotions are like the current that flows in those circuits.'

'Ohh ...'

'A woman is the embodiment of emotions and she feels most alive when emotions are supercharged in her brain. She loves experiencing these emotions, be it happiness, sadness, pain, pleasure, jealousy, or whatever. She feels almost dead when her life is devoid of these emotions.'

As I registered those words in my mind, I drifted into the past. I had always wondered why women were more emotional than men. I guess Krish's words explained that part. He hadn't finished speaking, so I waited to hear what he would say next.

'You know why I was laughing when that nice guy was proposing to that girl in the club?' Krish asked.

'Why?'

'Because I knew all along that she would reject him.'

'How did you know?'

'Well ...' Krish said and took a long pause, probably to consider how he could explain to me better. 'Girls don't want to experience just happiness. They like to experience a range of emotions. And they fall for guys who give them that.'

I listened to his words but had difficulty understanding what he meant.

'Can you please break that down for me?' I asked Krish.

'Sure,' he replied and continued, 'See, the nice guys give chocolates, flowers, gifts, and what not to girls. These things do make a girl *happy*.'

'Okay.'

'But flirts ... they make a girl happy by complimenting her on her beauty or praising her qualities or gifting her something occasionally. But they do something else too.' Krish paused for effect.

'What?' I wanted to know.

'A flirt sometimes avoids her completely and makes her feel rejected. Sometimes, he acts mysterious and confuses her.

Sometimes, he shouts at her in anger and hurts her. Sometimes, he hangs out with other girls and makes her jealous. Sometimes, he teases her playfully and embarrasses her. And sometimes ... you get the drift, right?'

'Kind of.'

'Well ... if you observe, a flirt gives a girl a range of emotions. He makes her experience happiness, sadness, jealousy, embarrassment, confusion, excitement, fear, pain, and a whole lot of emotions. And experiencing a wide range of emotions is what girls enjoy the most.'

I slowly began to understand what Krish was trying to say. The pieces of the puzzle were slowly falling into place. Even though I had a hunch, I still wanted Krish to put the rest of the pieces in place in order to give the complete picture. I asked him, 'Do you mean to say that a nice guy gives only happiness and the girl gets bored after a while? Whereas, a flirt makes her experience all kinds of emotions and keeps her guessing?'

'Right,' Krish said, putting his arm around my shoulder. I felt he was happy that he had finally got his point across. But he went on to explain to me in a little more detail.

'A girl has no control over who she gets attracted to and who she doesn't get attracted to. It's all emotions and no logic. So when she finds a guy who is able to give her so many emotions, she can't help but get attracted to him. So you should always remember to make a girl experience emotions rather than just trying to make her happy. That's where most guys fail,' Krish concluded.

As I listened to those words, it felt like the light had turned to my side. 'Point noted, Love Guru,' I said.

Krish fell silent for a minute. Then he sighed and said, 'Look, Arjun. Life is short and you gotta enjoy it to the fullest while it lasts. I know that you have seen worse in life and have experienced immense pain. But leave all that right now and look forward to a bright future.'

After Anjali, if there was anyone who showed so much concern for me, it was Krish. He wanted me to be happy. I felt blessed to have a friend like him. I hugged him and said, 'Thank you so much.'

'Stop this, man. It's dark here, and if someone sees us, they'll think we are gay,' he joked and laughed.

I laughed with him.

He then took out a cigarette and wrote three names on it – Shraddha, Neha, Saakshi. He asked me to smoke it. I did as he instructed and watched the three names burning slowly. At the end, when only the stub remained, Krish asked me to grind the stub under my shoe. I did it and felt relieved.

'The three girls who gave you pain and sorrow are gone now forever. You are not gonna think of them again, okay?' Krish said, putting his hand behind my neck.

I nodded in agreement.

How could someone enter your life and change it completely?

■

I went up to my room and changed into shorts and a t-shirt. I tried to sleep, but couldn't. I usually slept blissfully every time I got drunk, but Krish's words kept reverberating inside my head. They were more intoxicating than alcohol. All night, I kept staring at the ceiling in the dark and replayed everything that Krish had told me. I felt like I had been living in the dark all this while.

I walked out of my room after some time and rested on the beanbag, watching the full moon and bright stars. I was so lost in thought that I didn't realize when dawn arrived. When I saw the first light of the sun, I remembered Krish's last words, to leave the past and to move on towards a bright future. I got this urge to write a poem immediately.

I went inside my room hurriedly and penned down a few lines.

Sometimes when your life is filled with sorrow,
When everything around seems dark and hollow
Remind yourself that you are like an arrow
Pulled backwards momentarily for a better tomorrow.
The sun is rising and your life will be filled with light,
All the pain and darkness will be nowhere in sight.
Defeating your inner demons in the mighty fight,
You're gonna be a bird and soar a beautiful flight.

Ruchika

The next morning, I went to the office early. I stood inside the lift and as the doors were about to close, Ruchika entered at the last moment.

'Hi,' I said.

'Hi,' she said and stood beside me.

She then leaned towards me and whispered in my ear, 'Your zip is open!'

Fuck! I must have forgotten in my hurry. I moved my hand towards my crotch immediately and tried to zip up my pant. But to my surprise, the pant was already zipped.

I turned towards Ruchika with a confused look. She was smiling.

'I meant the zip of your bag,' she said naughtily.

I couldn't help but grin from ear to ear and we both ended up laughing together. What a way to start Monday morning!

When the lift stopped at our floor, Ruchika moved out and I followed her. She was wearing skin tight jeans and a blue tee. What an amazing figure she had! If only her face were prettier.

Ruchika and I walked towards our desks and settled in. She started working, but I couldn't focus much on work. It wasn't because of Ruchika's figure, but because I couldn't help but think about the conversation I had had with Krish. My mind was inundated with thoughts about women's minds, which was quite unusual, as guys are usually obsessed with women's bodies and rarely with their minds.

I left office early that day and as soon as I reached home, I began penning down my thoughts. I wrote whatever came to my mind. My mind processed information way faster than my hands could write, but I did not give up.

It's one thing to listen to someone's words and it's another thing to ponder upon them to understand them better. Putting things down helped me find a way through the labyrinth of my thoughts. After an hour or so, I had an idea of what was actually running in my mind and slowly the picture appeared to become clearer.

Over the next three weeks, I repeated the same activity every day. I would come home in the evening and write down my thoughts about my life in general and about women's psychology in particular. And the very next day, I would discuss them with Krish during the smoke break that we took every morning at around 11.30. Krish would listen to me with a lot of patience and would correct me whenever I went wrong in my interpretation. He was like a know-all teacher and I was like a diligent student. The discussions with him helped me understand women much better.

I also decided during the same time to focus on improving myself. I went to the gym religiously and did my best to enhance my physique. I also decided to change the way I presented myself to the world and felt the need to work on my emotions. I decided not to reveal the real me to people. I no longer wanted to live the life of an honest loser. I had had enough of being nice to every girl and getting nothing but pain in the end. Thanks to Krish, I realized that being a nice guy in this world is the surest way of going into the deadly friendzone, for it's the manipulative guys who always have girls by their side. I wanted to be the guy who gets girls. I wanted to be like

Krish. But deep inside, I knew I could never be like him. I had to find my own way to become what I wanted. So I chose to tread a better path – being innocently cunning with girls. I had a hunch it would work for me.

I had some idea about how I could become awesome in my life, but I wondered how I could expand my social circle. Then it struck me that Facebook could be used as a tool to build a social life. Though it was a virtual social circle, it worked as well as a real one. In some cases, even better. So I reactivated my Facebook account after a very long time and got in touch with a lot of my old friends, even though I was hardly interested in them. All I needed was a platform to showcase my awesomeness and thence become attractive automatically.

I began posting my little poems on Facebook. Most of them were about whatever confusion and understanding I had about love, lust, and life. They were funny and insightful at the same time and most people could relate to them. The content did attract a lot of people and they began noticing me. Likes, comments, and shares followed and I slowly started getting myself onto the right track.

Meanwhile, Ruchika and I became good friends. Since we worked on the same project, sat in the same cubicle, and practised for Kaagaz together, it was kind of inevitable that we should end up getting closer to each other.

We would take our coffee breaks in the evening together. In the beginning, our discussions revolved around office work and music. But in no time, they shifted to general things and then to our personal lives.

She told me about how she used to skip her tuitions as a teenager to attend music classes, about how her mother was always pestering her to get married, about how her father thought she was overambitious, about how she hated women bitching about frivolous things, and about everything she felt like telling me at that moment.

As I began spending time with Ruchika, I realized that she unpeeled her emotional self in layers. That's what most women do, I understood later. They keep telling you about themselves in steps and you can't help but wonder how much more is hidden deep inside their hearts. I also realized that women's emotions mimic a sine wave. Women go through various emotions in cycles and express them to people they are very comfortable with.

One day, during one of our usual coffee breaks, Ruchika was in a sad mood. When I asked her the reason, she said nothing. But after I prodded her a few times, she began opening up.

She spoke about her uncle who had molested her when she was a kid and how it kept haunting her once in a while. I didn't know what to do or say.

I had learnt from my findings that when girls tell guys about their problems, most likely, they don't really want a solution to their problem. All they want is someone who can listen to them without judging them. So I let her do all the talking as I sat listening to her patiently. And as I began to understand what she had gone through, I wondered how every single person was fighting some kind of inner demon in their lives.

After sharing her experience for an hour, Ruchika placed her hand on mine softly and said, 'Thanks for listening. I've never told this to anyone in my life.'

Though I felt good listening to her, I was a little surprised when she touched my hand. It was after a long time that I was experiencing the touch of a girl. I wondered if I could place my other hand on hers and say not to worry. But I lacked the courage. So I sat there silently, letting her hand rest on mine.

After some time, we went back inside. A part of my brain was still thinking about Ruchika. Though she had shared the reason for being low, I had a hunch that there was something else bothering her. I thought of asking her, but refrained from doing so, for I felt she would tell me sometime soon anyway.

A day later, Krish took Ruchika and me to the huddle room as we had to compose another song. The inter-corporate competition was only three months away and Krish didn't want to leave any stone unturned. The sooner the songs were done, the more the time to practise them, was Krish's logic.

We entered the room to find Golu and Chhotu already practising. Krish and Ruchika took a few minutes to set their instruments. Krish then told everyone that the song they were going to compose that day was about the feelings of a girl who had lost a guy she dearly loves. A song about her helplessness and about how she misses him. It was the opposite of the first song for which I had written lyrics for Kaagaz.

He played the tune first. Ruchika, Golu, and Chhotu caught up with him while I listened to the tune intently. I needed to write lyrics to match the mood and tune of the song.

An hour later, after registering the tune in my head, I left the room. I strolled around the office campus and went outside to have a smoke. Slowly, words began dancing inside my head and I had to arrange them according to the tune. Soon, the first draft of the song was ready. I jotted it in my phone and read it aloud later in the huddle room.

I can see your face,
But I can't see you anymore.
I can look into your eyes,
But I can't read them anymore.
You hold my hand,
But I don't feel the love anymore.

You touch my body,
But you don't touch my soul anymore.

The lyrics were simple on the surface, but had deep meaning within. Krish liked it and was quite happy. Golu and Chhotu expressed their approval by strumming the guitar and banging the drums, respectively.

I then looked at Ruchika. She was looking at me intently, but when our eyes met, she turned her face away and began adjusting the synthesizer. I noticed tears in her eyes, but they were gone in an instant. She did say the lyrics were good, but without looking at me.

Everyone practised for another hour and I went outside to write the rest of the song. I came back later and shared it with them. Soon the practice was over.

Krish, Golu, and Chhotu left for work, which left Ruchika and me in the room. She was packing the synthesizer. I walked up to her and asked her if she was okay.

'I am fine,' she said, trying to avoid eye contact. Her tone belied her words.

'You sure?' I said.

She remained silent, looking down, and said, 'I ... am ...'

'What happened?' I said, bending my head to look into her eyes. She raised her head and a stream of tears started rolling down her cheeks.

I was surprised.

She then did the unthinkable. She rushed towards me and hugged me, resting her head on my chest. She then began sobbing incessantly.

I didn't know what to do. I just let her be. She herself began speaking while her sobbing continued.

'I loved him so much, more than anything else in this world. I changed myself for him and did everything to keep him happy. But a few days ago ...' She paused and sobbed a little more and then continued, 'A few days ago, I found out that he was cheating on me with another girl.'

'Hmm.'

I didn't even know who she was talking about. I put my hand on her head, caressed her hair in slow strokes, and said, 'Don't worry. Everything will be okay.'

'I am deeply hurt, Arjun. I don't love him anymore. But the pain is killing me.'

'Hmm.' I continued stroking her hair.

She cried for some more time and then told me about her boyfriend. I listened to her as my T-shirt became wet with her tears, but I didn't really mind.

After like twenty minutes, she regained her composure slowly. I offered to drop her to her PG on my bike. She didn't say yes, but she didn't refuse either. She just walked along with me to the parking lot.

On the way to her PG, she was silent and didn't really say much. I noticed her in the rear-view mirror and she was staring into the void, most likely recollecting her past.

We reached her PG and before leaving she said, 'Sorry for the inconvenience.'

'You don't consider me your friend?' I said.

'I do, idiot!' she said, a little annoyed.

'They say no sorry in friendship,' I said, quoting one of the oldest dialogues ever in the history of friendship.

'Okay.' She tried to smile and said, 'Thanks for everything.'

'In friendship, no thanks too,' I said.

'Okay, sorry for saying thanks,' she said. And before I could say anything, she realized that she had now said sorry and thanks together in a single line. 'Aiyyoo,' she said, hitting her forehead.

I laughed and she smiled. I was happy I could make her smile.

She said bye and walked into her PG. I turned my bike and left for my room. Something was going to happen, I felt.

The next morning, after working out in the gym, Krish and I went to our usual hangout – the Dosa Palace. I told Krish what had happened with Ruchika and then began the usual discussion on women.

After listening to me for a while, Krish said, 'Stop!' putting his hand up like a traffic policeman at a junction. He continued, 'Enough theory, man. It's time for practicals!'

'But I am still trying to —'

'Ruchika,' Krish said, interrupting me.

'Ruchika??'

'Yeah, she seems to be on the verge of a break-up. It's a good time to make a move.'

As soon as Krish said that, Ruchika's image flashed before my eyes. She had an attractive figure but her face was just okay.

'I want my first time to be with a very beautiful girl,' I said to Krish.

Krish stopped eating and said, leaning forward, 'Tendulkar didn't play his first test match at Lord's.'

'Ohh.'

When I met Ruchika on Monday morning, she didn't seem as upset as she had been on Friday. When I asked her the reason, she said that she had cussed her boyfriend and had broken up with him. I was not sure if it was the right decision for her, but for me, it was, as I would know later.

Over the next month, Ruchika and I grew much closer to each other. When a guy and a girl start spending an awful lot of time together, they are bound to get attracted to each other. Maybe that's how Mother Nature works.

On the work front, Ruchika was extremely good at articulating clients' requirements and I was quite good at coding. We had to work together and we complemented each other. Even though we spent almost all day at office together, we couldn't stop ourselves from having long chatting sessions on WhatsApp after leaving office.

We shared YouTube video links of all-time favourite songs with each other. We loved each other's taste in music. We even recommended interesting books and movies to each other. And during one of those sessions, almost a month after she had hugged me while sobbing, she asked me to watch this movie called *Friends with Benefits*. I downloaded the movie but never really watched it.

One fine Saturday morning, we planned a trip to Wonder La – a water-based theme park on the outskirts of Bangalore. For the entire day, we enjoyed ourselves, taking those thrilling water rides and playing in the water. I don't know what the relation between water and sexual feelings is, but that day I did feel something for Ruchika. She was wearing nylon clothes that hugged her body after getting wet. Her figure was so sexy she'd give even Katrina Kaif a run for her money.

Ruchika began splashing water on me when we were in a swimming pool and I, in my attempt to dodge that, held her hand. She didn't stop and I involuntarily went behind her and held her by her waist. She didn't mind at all and instead enjoyed the act, which was quite evident from her expressions and her naughty smile. After spending the whole day together, we returned to the city.

'It was one of the best days of my life,' Ruchika said with a big smile when I dropped her at her PG late at night.

The next day, I took complete rest. But in the evening, Ruchika called me and said that she had booked tickets for a movie. I had no problem going with her, but the only thing that I hated was that the theatre was in the other end of town from Ruchika's PG. Which meant I had to first go to her PG, take a return trip till my room, and then drive to the theatre. Mathematically speaking, my room was the midpoint from Ruchika's PG to the theatre.

When I went to pick her up, she was dressed in faded blue denims and a cream colour tee.

I couldn't help but notice how hot she looked in that simple outfit. It was as if the jeans were custom-made for her, hugging her thighs and her calves perfectly. She looked sensuous. Maybe she was indeed looking hot or maybe my eyes were clouded with lust.

She came towards me and then, putting her hand on my shoulder, jumped on to my bike. I vroomed until we reached the theatre.

The movie began in some time and I rested my right hand on the armrest. Soon after, Ruchika placed her hand on the armrest too, nudging my elbow until I had no place at all to put my hand. I looked at her and she was smiling mischievously. I understood that she was doing it deliberately. So I too did the same, nudging her elbow using mine. She nudged mine in no time and I nudged hers again. It was like a game where we were jostling for a place on the armrest and we enjoyed it like two kids.

After a while, we came to a compromise. Ruchika said that we would entangle our elbows so that we both could rest our hands on the armrest. I was quite okay with that. But as the movie continued, my skin started tingling as I felt Ruchika's skin against mine. I was least interested in watching the movie.

I then moved my hand slowly and held Ruchika's fingers. She did not object. After playing with her fingers for a while, I entangled my fingers with hers. Her palms were soft unlike mine and it felt good.

Just before the interval scene, I removed my hand and then got up to bring popcorn and Coke. When I came back, Ruchika was smiling at me. I smiled back and gave her a cone of popcorn and sat down in my seat.

As I was eating popcorn from the cone in my hand, Ruchika threw some popcorn on my face. I turned towards her and she feigned ignorance. No sooner had I started eating again than she threw some more popcorn on me. I looked at her; she was trying to stifle her smile. I understood she was just playing another stupid game with me. So I joined her and started throwing popcorn at her. In no time, we went back to being two silly kids, throwing popcorn at each other. And after some time, Ruchika unloaded the entire cone on my head and I did the same to her. We couldn't stop laughing.

Thankfully, the movie began and we went back to holding each other's hands. After some time, I feigned a yawn and slowly rested my head on Ruchika's shoulder. She didn't move, which meant that she was okay with it. So I moved my head further and now my cheeks were resting on her shoulders. Her hair was now falling on my face and I was secretly hoping she wouldn't move. And she didn't.

I stayed in the same position till the movie ended. Throughout, she didn't move at all. Only once, her breathing got heavy and again went to normal after a minute.

As the movie ended, Ruchika shook me and I acted as if I was waking up from deep sleep. But I guess Ruchika had figured out that I hadn't really been asleep. She didn't mind though.

We headed home. It was late in the night and the weather was biting cold. There weren't many people on the road too and, refreshingly, there was no traffic in Bangalore at that hour of the night.

After a while, Ruchika began talking about how I had missed the best part of the movie. She went on explaining what had happened after the interval. I asked her to speak louder as I couldn't hear her properly because of the wind. But instead of speaking loudly, she leaned closer and continued talking about the movie. I couldn't concentrate on what she was saying because her breasts were now touching my back. I wondered if she was doing it intentionally.

Ruchika moved back after a while, but only for a few minutes. She brushed her boobs on my back again as she began talking. I went back in time and recollected that exactly the same incident had happened with Saakshi. She had then asked me to take her to my room on the pretext of booking train tickets. But I had been too stupid to read her mind.

Moreover, I remembered Krish's words that girls never tell anything directly and instead drop subtle hints. It's a guy's duty to decode those hints and decipher the meaning. So, this time, it didn't take long for me to understand Ruchika's feelings. I didn't want to miss a chance this time. I didn't want to be called a buddhu again.

As Ruchika continued talking, her breasts still touching my back, I wondered what I could do next. Krish had told me girls feel comfortable when they don't have to worry about privacy. I felt that no place in Bangalore would be more private than my room. But how could I take her to my room?

I kept thinking of some pretext, but my mind wouldn't come up with any ideas. And as we were nearing my room, Ruchika said, 'I am feeling hungry.'

'You won't find anything to eat at this time. It's already too late,' I said, unaware of her hidden intention.

'Your room is nearby, na. There must be something to eat,' she said innocently.

If I had been the same old loser Arjun, I would have felt that Ruchika was indeed hungry. But I was a changed person now. I understood the intention behind her words.

'Ya, there are some fruits in the fridge and a few Maggi packets in the kitchen,' I said.

'Maggi will do,' she said.

When we reached my house, Ruchika scanned everything around for a while. After washing her face in the washroom, she went to the kitchen and made Maggi. While she was doing that, I went to the washroom to calm down. I was tense, to be honest. But I didn't let it show on my face.

When I came back, Maggi was ready and Ruchika was sitting on the bed, leaning against the wall. She asked me to bring my laptop and sit beside her.

'Play some nice movie,' she said, as I made myself comfortable beside her.

I thought of playing songs that she had shared with me, but to my surprise, she stopped my hand and clicked on the folder 'Friends with Benefits'.

The movie was about a guy and a girl who have sex without being emotionally attached to each other. Ruchika played the movie.

Suddenly, my feet touched hers. She didn't move them away, but instead moved them closer. I realized it was time for me to make a move and take a chance.

But I remembered Krish's golden words. He had said that guys are like light bulbs. It doesn't take too much time for guys to get turned on or off. But girls are like iron boxes. It takes time for them to get heated up and then takes them time to cool down. So I told myself that I was going to take it slow, even though it was so hard to resist the temptation.

After finishing the Maggi, I put the plates in the kitchen, came back, and sat a little closer to her. I then did what I had done in the theatre – intertwined my fingers with hers and rested my head on her shoulder. She put her hand on my cheek. We watched the movie silently for some time. I squeezed Ruchika's hand tight when the hero and heroine began to kiss each other passionately and ended up having sex. We looked at each other with excitement.

I don't remember if I moved closer to her or she did, but we closed our eyes and our lips met.

God! It was the first time in my life that I was kissing a girl on her lips. Even though I had watched kissing scenes in movies many times, I can't tell you how difficult it is to kiss properly for the first time. I was a fresher, but Ruchika was experienced, for she had had a boyfriend for years. So she took the lead and began sucking my lips. I reciprocated whatever she did. Damn! Her lips were soft like rose petals and I became a honeybee, trying to suck nectar from them.

She entangled her tongue with mine. And then slowly moved it just over my teeth and I felt a tingling sensation running from my neck down the spine. My hands involuntarily moved towards her waist. And like a moth drawn to the flame, my fingers glided towards her breasts. But she held my wrists with her hands and stopped me from going ahead. Thankfully, she didn't stop kissing.

We kissed each other for a few more minutes and then stopped to catch our breath. It didn't last long as we went back to kissing each other again. This time, Ruchika began kissing more passionately, with her hands running through my hair just above the neck. She kept pulling my hair occasionally.

It suddenly dawned on me that since her hands were now busy, I could try again to rest my hands on her waist and move them upwards. I don't know how I figured it out, but I felt that the best way to remove a girl's tee was to keep her so engrossed in the kiss that her inhibitions to remove her clothes would reduce considerably. I did the same and it worked.

I then tried to unhook her bra, but I couldn't. No matter how hard I tried, the hooks just wouldn't budge.

Ruchika started laughing at my struggle. She put her right hand behind and within a nanosecond undid her bra. I removed it from her body to see the amazing sight of her naked breasts. They were small though, but it didn't really matter at the moment. In no time, we undressed each other and had sex. And ... I lost my virginity!

Half an hour later, we lay on the bed, side by side, facing the ceiling. We were exhausted and completely spent. I was on top of the world and felt liberated.

Ruchika got up and put on her bra. She then pulled the quilt, lay beside me, and covered both of us. I extended my arm on the pillow and Ruchika rested her head on it, playing with the hair on my chest with one hand.

'So, how did you feel?' she asked me.

'Well ...' I tried to find the right words to describe the feeling, but I just couldn't.

'I fall short of words to describe how heavenly this feeling is. It's like jumping off a cliff and then floating in the air for a long time and then landing slowly on a bed of green grass,' I said.

'When a lyricist says he is short of words to describe something, it indeed means something special.' Ruchika smiled.

'Hmm,' I said, my hand now moving over from her neck to her back.

We then fell silent for a few minutes. I was replaying the scene that had just happened and a strange kind of tranquillity filled my mind.

'Say something na,' Ruchika said.

I turned my head towards her slowly and said, my hands still roving over her back, 'Why don't they manufacture bras without hooks?'

'Idiot!' she said, slapping my face playfully.

After that night with Ruchika, my life changed. And for the next two months, I had the time of my life with her. She would come to my room twice or thrice a week and we would end up spending all night together, watching movies and having sex. One good thing was that the sex was casual and we never gave any name to our relationship. We would never talk about unnecessary topics like love, marriage, and the future. We were just living in the moment and having a lot of fun.

I learnt the basics of sex with Ruchika. It was an altogether different experience, something that made me feel alive like nothing else.

I became more mature during this time. I began to understand that most women aren't as innocent or sweet as they pretend to be. There is a stark difference between the woman in bed and the one in public. For example, Ruchika, who would stay aloof in the office, would shed all her inhibitions in bed and crave for my touch. It felt like I was discovering an entirely new person in her.

As time passed, I didn't know that the best in life, other than sex, was still to come. Ruchika and I, after romping with each other for two whole months, started focusing on the inter-corporate competition, which was only a month away. During that time, we met in my room only during weekends.

During weekdays, most of the time we were with Krish, Golu, and Chhotu, completely focused on creating magic with soul-stirring songs. Even though I had already written lyrics for all the six songs, I kept tweaking the lyrics, trying to make them as beautiful as possible. It's amazing how a simple rearrangement of a few words or the addition of one right word can add to the beauty of the song significantly. While Kaagaz practised behind closed doors, I would write lyrics in my mind during my long strolls around the office. I would come back once in a while and recite the lyrics to the band. Krish would suggest some changes and the cycle would continue.

By the time the competition neared, we were all geared up. Now, it was only a matter of time before Kaagaz performed at the event.

On D-day, as expected, Kaagaz rocked the show. Our performance was nothing short of sizzling. Krish was on fire, while Ruchika, Golu, and Chhotu supplied the wind. All four of them were magnificent.

They played only three of the six songs because of time constraints. The last one was about the frivolity of love and how lust precedes love in modern-day relationships. The song resonated well with the young audience and they went crazy. Once Krish was done singing the song, everyone in the audience began shouting 'Once more'. Kaagaz obliged and this time the audience too joined in. Loud applause followed.

When the time to announce the prizes came, the whole auditorium was chanting 'Kaagaz! Kaagaz!' The judges didn't disappoint. We won the first prize and I was beyond ecstatic. I was standing in the audience as I watched Krish, Ruchika, Golu, and Chhotu take the prize. I was clapping incessantly.

Krish took the mike and thanked everyone for the support. He then did the unthinkable. He said that one of the main reasons for their victory was the lyrics written by me. He asked me to come on the stage. 'Please give a big round of applause for Arjun,' Krish said, as people made way for me. I went up the stage and he hugged me. Ruchika, Golu, and Chhotu joined us and we all bear-hugged each other and jumped like kids.

But then, there was another surprise in store for me. The judges began announcing prizes for best guitarist, best keyboard player, and the likes. And then, they announced the best lyricist award.

'Arjun,' the judge called my name and I was pleasantly surprised. Ruchika high-fived and Krish hugged me again. I slowly made my way to collect the award. The feeling was indescribable, watching myself collect an award in front of such a large audience.

Tears of happiness were ready to fall, but I blinked my eyes and they disappeared.

I don't know why, but at that moment I wanted some solitude. So I excused myself from everyone and went behind the auditorium, strolling in the lawn, recalling the first time I had written a poem after I was rejected by Neha and then remembering all the nights that I had spent trying to weave words into poems. The journey now seemed quite fulfilling.

I was lost in a haze of thoughts, but was interrupted when someone tapped my shoulder from behind. I turned to see a chubby girl with wavy hair and a nose ring. She was smiling at me as I checked her out without her knowledge.

She was wearing a black scoop-neck t-shirt, with the strap of her sling bag resting between her huge breasts. They were protruding, and for a minute I felt the urge to free them out of the prison of her t-shirt. Beneath, she was wearing a long, light-blue and white pleated skirt resembling the sky.

'Hey,' she said, extending her hand.

'Hello.' I held her hand.

'Congratulations for the award! The lyrics were indeed very heartfelt and quite evocative,' she said, shaking my hand.

'Thanks,' I replied.

'I am Esha, a journalist working for City Life edition of a popular newspaper. I am here to cover the event.'

'I see.'

'I was wondering if you have a few minutes so that I can take a short interview.'

'Sure,' I said.

'Can we sit there?' she said, pointing to a bench, and we went there and made ourselves comfortable.

She took out a book and a pen from her bag and began asking questions like what inspired me to write songs and other such questions that lyricists are usually asked. I answered all of them candidly.

'Thank you so much,' she said as she got up. 'I need your number, just in case I need any more information while writing the article.'

'Sure,' I said and gave her the number. Seconds later, my phone started vibrating. I guessed it was the journo who had made a call, but the call was from Anjali. I looked at the phone and then at the journo, deliberating if I should pick up the call or take it later. But Esha whispered bye, smiled, and walked away. I answered the call.

'Hii,' Anjali said.

'Heyy.'

'How did the inter-corporate competition go, mister? I didn't disturb you all these days guessing you must be busy with the preparations.' So she had remembered the event date and cared to ask me what had happened.

'It went well. In fact, I won the best lyricist award,' I said, trying to be casual.

'Woowww. Congrats, hero! That's so amazing.'

'Yeah ... I guess.'

'Where are you right now?' she said, pausing before saying the words 'right' and 'now', for effect.

'Still near the venue.'

'Can you meet me now? Like right now.'

'Sure,' I said, realizing that I hadn't met her in a long time.

I met Krish, Ruchika, Golu, and Chhotu backstage. They wanted to celebrate the success. I excused myself, saying I needed to meet a friend. They made a big fuss, but they did let me go in the end.

I met Anjali at a restaurant and she was very excited. She asked me every minute detail about the event and I couldn't help but narrate to her like an author narrating a scene from his book. I was happy, but I didn't know why Anjali was way happier than me. Her excitement was so evident that I wondered if people around us would think she had won a jackpot.

After listening to me for a while, Anjali began talking about her hectic life as a medico. There was a lot to catch up on and Anjali had this art of interlacing even her sob stories with humour. So I never felt bored listening to her. But for a moment, I did feel guilty for ignoring her for the past two months. She had called me twice or thrice and I was busy having fun with Ruchika. I had lied to Anjali though, saying I was busy with the preparations for the competition. It was, as far as I could remember, the first time I was lying to her, for I had never really hidden anything from her. I wasn't sure how she would take it if I told her about Ruchika. So I felt it was better to keep it under wraps.

An affair should be like a password. You should have one, but you shouldn't let the world know about it!

The very next morning, I got a call from Anjali while I was fast asleep. She was more ecstatic than she had been the previous day, the reason being an article about me in the newspaper.

I spoke to her nonchalantly on the phone as my sleep was getting the better of me at the moment. She spoke for some time about how happy she was to see the article and disconnected after a while, not because she was done, but because she had to go see an ailing patient in the hospital.

When I woke up fully, I went to a nearby stationery shop without even brushing my teeth. I bought the newspaper and flipped to the City Life edition. It was for the first time in my life that I was seeing myself in a newspaper. I thought how happy Mom and Dad would have been if they had been alive. That day, I missed them a lot.

After a few moments of silence, I went on reading what was written and I must say that the article was written quite impressively. 'I write from my heart' was the caption beneath my pic. I took a snap of it and posted it on Facebook, not because I wanted to share my happiness with everyone, but because I wanted to improve my awesomeness quotient.

I felt like thanking Esha, but I didn't have her contact details. Luckily, I found her email id at the end of the article. And the first thing I did after going to the office was write an email to her, thanking her for making me feel like a mini-celebrity. I was hoping for a reply from her, but I didn't get any. She lingered for a week at the back of my mind.

Tequila, weed and cocaine

On a Monday afternoon, I got a call from an unknown number. I answered the call and recognized the husky voice instantly.

'Hi, this is Esha,' she said.

'Hii,' I said, excitement evident in my voice.

'What's up?'

'These days everything in my life is up,' I said trying to sound cool, but regretted it immediately as it sounded somewhat silly.

'Nice ... You busy now?'

'No, no. Tell me,' I said, even though there was a lot of work pending.

'I am outside your office. Just thought we could meet up.'

'Really? I will be there in two minutes,' I said, shutting down my laptop and running hurriedly towards the lift lobby.

I saw her outside the gate under a tree, sitting on a Honda Activa, wearing a helmet without a visor. I went up to her, smiled broadly, and said, 'Hii.'

'Hello, Mr Lyricist.'

I smiled and said, 'How are you?'

'Fine ... Come, sit,' she said, pointing to the pillion. I liked her confidence.

'Where are we going?' I asked as I sat on her bike happily, my knees touching her thighs. She didn't mind. She didn't answer my question, and started her bike.

'Thanks for the article. A lot of people have suddenly started admiring me. I got a lot of messages on Facebook from many people,' I said, trying to break the silence.

'Hmm' was all she said and I wondered why she wasn't saying anything at all.

I too remained silent until she stopped at a coffee shop and I got down. Putting the helmet beneath the seat, she said, 'I can drive a car easily. But thanks to the Bangalore traffic, I bought this Activa recently as I find it more convenient. Since I am new to this bike, I can't for the life of me drive properly if I keep talking.'

That explained why she had been silent all the while.

'Come, let's go inside,' she said, pointing to the coffee shop.

'Sure,' I said. And then, I opened the door for her, showing some chivalry. She smiled at my gesture.

We walked towards a corner table and made ourselves comfortable. She rested her hands and then her breasts on the table.

'So you are around on some work?' I initiated the conversation.

'Yeah. I came here to interview the head of a technology start-up. I need to write an article on entrepreneurship,' she said.

'Is that all?' I asked, curious to know why she had sought *me* out.

'Well, not really. I am writing another article on love affairs in corporate offices in Bangalore and I needed to talk to someone who can give me inside information about what goes on behind the glass walls of these plush offices,' she said casually.

'Okay,' I said, still wondering why of all the people in Bangalore she chose me.

'I am new to this city and I don't really know a lot of people here. It suddenly struck me that I can take your help,' she said, clearing the doubt in my mind.

'Ohh. Where are you from?' My inquisitiveness got the better of me.

'From Delhi.'

'So you live here in a PG?'

'No, my grandparents left a huge house for us in Bangalore. I live there alone. My parents live in the US and I will be going there in a few months.'

'For higher studies?'

'Yup! I want to do my master's in political science and international strategy. It's my dream to become a war correspondent someday,' she said, her voice oozing confidence.

'So what exactly do you want from me?' I said, bringing back the conversation to the reason she had met me.

'Yeah, I want you to tell me about the affairs in your office. Whether people are open about it or maintain a lot of secrecy. Whether affairs are very common or quite rare. And about everything that you think I need to know to write a good, spicy article.'

I smiled at her questions and she smiled back. I then went on to tell her how affairs in the office are almost always hushed. Freshers who join the company, with their bodies raging with hormones, form a major chunk. But a few couples end up in committed relationships and get married. Most have fun till it lasts. Some elderly men, bored of their nagging wives and responsibilities, do end up hooking up with young girls in the office. Conversely, some young girls like older men because they find the guys of their age too immature. I told her about all this in detail.

'You are not in a relationship?' she asked in a casual tone.

'Well ...' I paused and said, 'I am. It's a recent one.'

'You can tell me about that,' she said, without mincing any words.

'There is this girl in my office ...' I said and told her almost everything about my affair with Ruchika. I changed events and places, and made sure not to let out Ruchika's name throughout, just to maintain privacy. When I ended up talking about the sex, Esha was smiling naughtily. I couldn't help but ask her what happened.

'Nothing. Your story reminds me of an affair I had with a guy in Delhi,' she said, blinking her eyes.

'So you had a boyfriend in Delhi?'

'Boyfriends actually,' she said, with a mischievous smile.

'Now that's something,' I said, mimicking her smile.

'Yeahh. Relationships are just not my thing.' She paused for a while and then said, 'You see, almost every Indian guy wants a girl who thinks about him all the time, cooks for him, and takes care of him every day. Who wants to marry an ambitious girl dreaming of becoming a war correspondent someday?'

'True.'

'Love can wait, but dreams can't. But still, the body has its needs, right? We are young, crazy, and full of life. So why not have some fun while working hard for our dreams at the same time?'

I looked at her in wonder and couldn't help but get attracted to her killer attitude. She raised her eyebrows, asking me, 'What?'

'Nothing. You're the best,' I said, giving her a thumbs-up. She smiled.

Esha then dropped me to the office. As soon as I reached my desk, Ruchika asked me where I had been. 'Just ... just went out to meet an old friend,' I lied to her. She didn't bother asking the details.

I tried to finish my work, but I couldn't concentrate. Esha's words kept ringing in my head. The conversation I had had with her was something that one doesn't have every day. Moreover, it was quite unbelievable that we had met for the first time. It was like we had known each other since forever.

I went home and deliberated over calling her. I found the courage eventually and dialled the number. But she didn't pick up my call. Fuck!

I didn't know what it was that attracted me to Esha. Maybe it was her fleshy body or maybe her sexy attitude, but I couldn't help but think about her most of the time. I thought of calling her again, but I dropped the idea as I felt I would sound needy and desperate. So I waited for her call. And good heavens, she did call me, although after a week.

'Hi Arjun,' she said.

'Hey. How have you been?'

'I have some good news for you.' Esha liked coming to the point directly, I understood.

'Tell me,' I was curious.

'Well ... an upcoming director has sent me an email. Apparently, he read the article about you winning the inter-corporate competition and he wants to sign you up for a film.'

'Really?' I almost shouted in excitement.

'Yeah. He wants to meet you this weekend.'

'Done!'

On Saturday, Esha and I went to meet the director. He welcomed us warmly. He said that he was planning to make a youth-oriented movie and was looking for some fresh talent to write lyrics. He stressed on the word fresh and I understood why I had been called. I agreed without even thinking twice. You don't get such offers every day!

After leaving his home, Esha and I stopped at a nearby paan shop. She bought two cigarettes and offered one to me. Even though I was a bit startled, it felt incredibly sexy to watch the super-confident girl smoking casually.

'Thanks,' I said to her, for it was her article that had got me the movie offer.

'That's okay.'

'I owe you a treat for this at least,' I said. I really wanted to return her favour.

'Well ...'

'When will you be free?'

'Let's go now,' she said, without even asking for my approval.

'Now?'

'Ya. Life is short. Why wait till tomorrow when you can have fun today?' She drew me more into her with that line.

We rode to a relatively obscure pub near Koramangala. The only light in the pub came from the spotlight on the stage. There was a mike too and I would know later it was for karaoke.

We sat in the dark on two barstools and she ordered tequilas for both of us, without even asking me whether I liked it or not. I liked her dominating nature for some strange reason. When the bartender gave us the glasses, we said cheers and drank up in one go. It tasted bitter and I hung my tongue out in disgust. Esha began laughing because she understood it was the first time I had tasted a tequila. She said we should have a few more shots and I said yes, licking some salt and lemon. We had another shot and I felt dizzy. Another round of shots and I began to experience the high.

Soon, the DJ began playing music. Enthusiastic boys and girls sang songs of their choice. Music from A.R. Rahman's *Rangeela* was being played and, all of a sudden, Esha rushed to the stage. She held the mike in her hands and began singing, reading out the lyrics from the screen.

Tanha tanha yahaan pe jeena,
ye koi baat hai
Koi saath nahi tera yahaan toh,
Ye koi baat hai.

She moved her body seductively while singing. Her head moved in rhythm and her hair rose and fell like waves in an ocean. She then came back, all excited, and coerced me to go on the stage and sing a song. I wouldn't have had the courage to sing if it weren't for the alcohol in my system. I sang hoarsely and some people booed. Esha clapped all the while though and when I came back she said, 'One should never really care what others think and should always do whatever one likes.'

'Yo!' I said to her as we gulped down one more shot.

Esha then began telling me about her affairs, seven of them, and how much she had enjoyed the sexcapades. She told me in detail about the naughty stuff that she had done. The details were so explicit that I had a hard-on just by listening to her.

When she asked me about my affairs, I told her that I had had three affairs. I was obviously lying as I didn't want to sound like a loser. I made up stories about my shenanigans with my imaginary girlfriends. I did add a few racy details and Esha enjoyed them too, which was evident from her naughty smiles and hysterical laughs.

Another shot of tequila, and I felt a twirling in my stomach. Before I could hold myself, I threw up. It was very embarrassing, to say the least. But strangely, Esha didn't mind at all. She assisted me till the door of the men's washroom and waited until I came out. I didn't realize I was so drunk that I could barely walk.

Esha helped me walk out of the pub. She drove the bike very slowly after I planted my butt on the pillion. I was too high to even sit properly. So I rested my head on her back and put my hands around her waist. Since the alcohol was out of my system now, I managed to give her directions to my room.

I got down and Esha assisted me upstairs. As we reached the last step, she put her hand in my pocket to take out the keys and opened the door. She made me lie on the bed as she thought I was still high, but then she tripped herself and fell on me.

Now, maybe it was the effect of the alcohol on that cold night, the chemistry between us, or the raging hormones, we began to kiss each other. I don't remember clearly as to what happened later, but we woke up in each other's arms in the morning, stark naked!

'Send me a photograph of yours,' she said, playing with my hair.

'Why?'

'Just send it, man. Not on WhatsApp, but to my email id,' she said. I took out my phone and emailed her a decent pic of mine. She saw the pic and smiled. We hugged each other and I went back to sleep again, as I was still hung over.

When I woke up after an hour, Esha had left. I called on her mobile but, as usual, she didn't pick up. I got up from the bed and freshened up. I tried to recollect whatever had happened the previous night.

When Krish had told me that women act on mood, I had believed him. But I was somewhat sceptical as to how a girl could sleep with a guy within a week of meeting him. But after the experience with Esha, all my doubts were cleared. Compatibility, chemistry, and timing were all that mattered, I understood.

Also, I recalled his dating formula to get girls – be awesome and mingle with people. Winning the best lyricist award had made me somewhat awesome, and if I hadn't won it, I would have been just another guy for Esha and she wouldn't even have known me. As I began to experience first-hand what Krish had tutored, I realized how amazing a guy Krish was. *How would my life have been if I hadn't met him?*

I spent the whole Sunday lazing around. But the next morning, I got a call from Anjali. She congratulated me for bagging the contract to write lyrics for a feature film.

'How do you know?' I asked her. I hadn't told anyone.

'I read the article today in City Life,' she said and read the headline – 'Techie Who Won Inter-Corporate Competition Gets Offer from Top Director. You are looking so good in the pic,' she said.

I thanked her, spoke to her for a while, and headed out to see the article. I understood why Esha had asked for the pic. She had already decided to write the article. I wanted to call her right away, but I knew she wouldn't answer. So I just sent her a message saying thanks. She didn't reply.

I got a call from her after two days. She asked me if I was free during the weekend. I think she knew I would say yes and was asking as a formality.

When I said I had nothing much to do on the weekend, she told me to come over to her home on Friday evening itself. She even told me to bring my nightwear along so that we could pull an all-nighter. She said she had something special in mind. I guess I knew what was coming.

During a coffee break, Ruchika asked me what was cooking between Esha and me, as she knew about the articles. I reiterated that Esha was just a friend.

'I am not your girlfriend. So I won't nag like one,' she said. 'What's the plan tonight?'

'Depends on what's your plan tonight,' I said and winked. Needless to say, I had a good time with Ruchika that night, but at the back of my mind, I was looking forward to spending the weekend with Esha. Sex with Ruchika was good, but good is good only for some time. You want amazing after that.

Friday evening came around and I was as excited as a kid going to a park filled with fun rides. The word 'ride' now had a different meaning though.

I drove to the address she had sent in Koramangala. When I reached there, I was quite taken in by her luxurious home. For a moment, I felt out of place.

I rang the doorbell and was awestruck as soon as she opened the door. She was wearing a lavender satin nightie with thin white shoulder straps. The hem of the gown was way above her knees, exposing her thighs entirely. 'Come,' she said, as I followed her inside the house.

The drawing room had classy cushion sofas, a coffee table, and a fluffy carpet covering the floor. It was separated from the hall by an arched curtain. As I walked, I noticed a huge LED TV and two beanbags. The ceiling had a beautiful chandelier and the walls were decorated with artificial flowers and leaves. Esha led me to the dining room. There were aluminium foil packets on the dining table which contained takeaway food. On the far end were a few packets with a tobacco-like substance.

'Hungry?' Esha asked as I sat on a chair at the dining table.

'Yes,' I said and winked. She understood the sexual innuendo behind my yes and flashed a naughty smile.

She went to the kitchen and brought two plates and served food. As she sat down on the chair, I noticed her breasts. Her gown had a V-shaped lacy neckline and it revealed her deep cleavage. As we began conversing, I couldn't help but stare at it once in a while. I was least interested in having dinner. The hard-on inside my pant was becoming unbearable and I was waiting to pounce on her breasts. Esha noticed my discomfort and smiled. I don't understand what pleasure girls get by making guys crave for them.

She put her hand below my chin, raised my head, and said, 'Look into my eyes.'

'It's difficult,' I confessed.

'Just wait for some time,' she said.

We finished our dinner and she took the plates into the kitchen as I went to the sink to wash my hands.

'Come,' she said, and held my hand and I followed her like a puppy. The house was a duplex and the stairs led to the bedrooms.

As I was walking behind her on the stairs, I noticed that she wasn't wearing any underwear. The sexy arc that formed between her hips and her fleshy thighs was a treat for the eyes. My hand was involuntarily moving towards her hips but I snatched it back.

As the stairs ended, a king-size bed welcomed us. It had a spring mattress with a white bed cover, two cushy pillows, and a brown quilt. The entire room was dimly lit and a bedside lamp added to the aesthetic appeal.

I turned towards Esha, and in an instant she pushed me onto the bed. I fell on my back, surprised. She then climbed over me and sat on my crotch, her legs astride. The sight of her fulsome breasts right in front of my eyes was titillating. I held her by the waist as she bent over me and began kissing me. She sucked my lower lip first and bit it gently. I felt some insane pleasure in that acute pain. Thanks to my experience with Ruchika, I now knew how to kiss.

I sucked Esha's upper lip all the while and we then began smooching, our tongues entangling, and battling for space in each other's mouths. We continued kissing for about fifteen minutes. Esha stopped when I was trying to move my hands from her waist towards her breasts.

She held both my wrists with her hands and flashed a wicked smile. She wasn't going to allow me so soon, I understood. She began kissing again and, after a while, she moved her lips to my chin. And then to my neck and towards my slightly hairy chest. She began to unbutton my shirt. She undid two buttons patiently and then tore open my shirt, the remaining buttons flying around. She continued kissing and grazed her lips over my chest and twirled her tongue over my belly button. I was ecstatic and barely able to hold myself.

I tried to free my hands and get hold of her breasts, but in vain. She pinned my hands over my head and leaned forward. She dangled her breasts right in front of my face and I lifted my head to bite one of them. But she didn't let me do it as she moved her breasts up too. I was now as impatient as a wolf waiting for the right time to jump on its prey. I wrestled with her for some time and succeeded after a while. I put my hands on her breasts and fondled them, her nipples between my forefinger and thumb. She raised her head towards the ceiling and moaned in ecstasy. I continued fondling.

She removed my hands in haste. She crossed her hands downwards, held the hem of her satin gown, and removed it in an instant. Very quickly, she unbuckled my belt, pulled my pants down, and freed my manhood. Before I realized, she began playing with the joystick, twirling her tongue over it and sucking those ping pong balls. I dug my head into the pillow and arched my body as a shiver ran throughout me. I didn't know that a blowjob could be so pleasurable.

After a few minutes, she sat on my shaft and let it trespass her velvety softness. She rocked to and fro, entangling her fingers with mine. I felt her wetness. The friction that was being caused as she increased the pace was heavenly. I closed my eyes and began rejoicing in elation. After a few minutes, my body felt an inexplicable pulsation, my toes twitched, and I came inside her. My heartbeat was so loud that I could hear it. My breathing grew heavy too and I just lay on the bed devoid of energy.

Esha was not done yet and I felt a little embarrassed. She didn't mind though, as she smiled at my predicament. She went downstairs and I wondered what she was up to. She came back after a while, with the pouch containing the tobacco-like substance in one hand and a pair of dice in the other.

She sat on the bed and asked me to relax until the next session. When I asked her what was in the pouch, she said, 'Weed.'

Okay, she was not just into cigarettes and alcohol, but also into weed. I watched her keenly as she made a joint. She lit up one and we smoked in turns. She rolled another one and we smoked that too.

Now, this was the thing about weed that I didn't know. For a few minutes, nothing really happened. But like slow poison, the high began to kick in. I suddenly felt as light as a feather. For no particular reason, I felt a rush of excitement and was fucking happy. I saw Esha and she was smiling at me, as if she knew all along that this was going to happen.

Esha grazed her fingers over my shoulders and arms. She said, holding my somewhat flabby abs, 'I like your shoulders and you have good arms. You must focus on the abs.' The workout at the gym had begun to amount to something, I told myself. She continued grazing her fingers on my arms and then my chest. I didn't know why I felt extra-sensitive to her touch then, but realized later it was because of the weed.

I held Esha tight and just as I was about to plant a kiss, she stopped me by putting her hand over my mouth. She got up and took the pair of dice in her hands. On one dice were places in the house – drawing room, bedroom, washroom, kitchen, dining room, and garage. The other dice, to my utter surprise, had six sex positions imprinted on it. It took me a while to guess her intentions as she explained the game.

We would roll the dice and based on the combination, we would have sex in various positions in different locations inside the house. Mathematically, there were thirty-six possibilities, I calculated mentally.

An engineer can never stop being an engineer!

We began the game and, thanks to weed, we played it all through the night. It began with 69 on the carpet in the drawing room and ended in the missionary position in the bathtub. We fell into a blissful sleep sometime around dawn. The night was unforgettable.

I was woken up late in the afternoon by pangs of hunger. Lunch was ready when I went downstairs. Esha was still nude.

We had food and continued playing the game over the weekend, with occasional breaks of course. The weed got us going and sex with Esha was an out-of-the-world experience. We were naked all the while, doing only three things – eating, sleeping, and fucking.

On Monday morning, as I woke up beside Esha, she said that it was the best sex she had ever had. She kissed me and said that it was very liberating. I believed her in spite of a few apprehensions, but I wondered why she had chosen me of all the people in Bangalore. She was a journalist and she sure would have had many contacts.

When I asked her, she replied, 'Trust.'

'What?' I was confused.

'Yeah. When you told me about the affair with the girl in your office, you didn't tell me her name in spite of me prodding you.'

'So?'

'So I became sure that whatever happens between us, you wouldn't tell anyone about it,' she clarified.

'Ohh,' I said, less because of her statement and more because I recollected what Krish had said. He had said that girls judge you by how you act in different scenarios and form conclusions based on your behaviour in various situations. A simple act of not revealing someone's identity had helped me get laid.

'No matter how much of a nymphomaniac a girl is, she does care about her reputation in society. I do, too. I am sure you will keep this a secret,' she said.

'Of course, I will,' I said.

Soon after I left for office from her home.

On the way, I reminisced how I had spent the weekend. It was, without any doubt, the best weekend I had ever had. The pleasure, the euphoria, and the exhilaration was unmatched. I had forgotten the entire world for two days, revelling in the pleasures of lust. It was like I didn't want to come back to reality. Esha, for me, was an escape from reality. And I became, for her, a stairway to heaven.

When I reached office, Krish observed my tired eyes and said, 'I guess you had a very busy weekend.'

'Yeahh,' I said, smiling mischievously. He winked at me, guessing very well what I had been up to.

After checking emails, we went for our usual smoke break and I told him everything about the weekend. When I told him that I was the eighth guy in her life, he interrupted me and said, 'Did you use protection?'

'No, but ...' I was more enthusiastic about telling him about the game I played with Esha. But he interrupted me again, took out two condoms from his wallet, and said, 'Look. From now on, no matter what, you are always going to use protection, okay?' He looked serious as he put them in my wallet.

'Okay,' I said.

'Continue,' he said, taking a puff of his cigarette.

I went on to tell him the rest of the story and he seemed quite happy with my accomplishment. That's the thing with guys. Unlike girls who usually feel a twinge of jealousy, most guys actually feel quite happy when their friend gets laid.

After I was done, he smiled and said, putting his hand on my shoulder, 'You are just a few steps from understanding the meaning of love, lust, and life.'

His line seemed a little out of context and I wondered what he really meant by that. But I didn't ask him. Though Krish had told me a million things about his life, I always wondered if there was something he kept to himself. He did seem quite mysterious sometimes.

When I went back to the desk, Ruchika was waiting for me. There was some pending work and she wanted me to finish it soon. And for the next few hours, I focused on coding and finished it by late evening. No matter what I did in life, be it working out in the gym, writing lyrics, or having fun with girls, if there was one thing which I never took lightly, it was my work in the office. I knew it was my bread and butter. Without a well-paying job, I wouldn't be able to enjoy other things in life.

In the evening, when I went for a coffee break with Ruchika, she asked me about my weekend.

'You didn't answer my calls,' she said.

'I was busy writing lyrics. I don't want to take this opportunity of working for a feature film lightly. I want to give my best,' I lied.

Maybe she guessed I was lying. But she didn't ask anything. And well, that's another unspoken rule of the 'friends with benefits' relationship, I realized. You can claim rights over someone's body, but you can't claim rights over their lives, decisions and soul.

It didn't affect our relationship though, for we slept together the very next day. It's just that my interest in Ruchika was slowly beginning to wane. You can't watch the same movie again and again, no matter how much you like it. I began to understand why marriages fail and why people lose interest in their spouses over a period of time.

For the next three days, I worked hard, both in the office and in the gym. I wanted to get six-pack abs so I could flaunt them the next time I met Esha. But it wasn't that easy to get perfect abs and I realized it would take its own sweet time. But I had to keep going.

Friend request

On a Saturday morning, after a strenuous workout, I took a selfie of my bare chest and arms, without focusing on the abs, and posted it on Facebook. More than two hundred likes and three dozen comments followed. I wasn't a sucker for likes and comments, but I enjoyed that, simply because it served as a social proof of my awesomeness. It amazed me how the world judges the worth of someone by the number of likes and comments that one gets.

I rested the whole day and checked my account late in the evening. I replied wittily to some of the comments posted. But then, just when I was about to log out, I got a friend request from a pretty girl. I saw her profile and my eyes widened in amazement. An inexplicable joy rushed through my body. I jumped out of my bed and did a mini-jig when I figured out who it was.

I spent the next half hour checking her profile. There were hundreds of pics and all of them had hundreds of likes. She really deserved that, for she was extremely beautiful. Most of the pics were taken at drunken parties in dim-lit pubs, but her ravishing looks shone through even the dim lighting. I took a screenshot of her friend request and then lay on my bed in elation.

There are moments in life that happen only once. They give you some kind of stupid joy and, though it may sound crazy to the rest of the world, the moment remains special to you. Getting a friend request from a childhood crush is one such moment. And yes, the friend request was from none other than my first crush – Aditi.

Though I was itching to accept her request, I refrained from doing so, for I realized I would seem too easy. She was extremely pretty and it was evident that she would have a lot of fans. I didn't want to be one of them. So, I delayed accepting her request.

When I checked my Facebook account the next evening, I saw three notifications. All three were from Aditi. She had liked posts on my timeline – about my winning the inter-corporate competition, about the offer from a movie director, and my topless selfie. What timing!

I accepted her friend request late at night, for I was afraid she might just cancel it if I delayed further. I wanted to say hi to her, but I didn't, again for the same reason, to not seem too easy. I knew somehow that she would initiate the conversation. And she did, after a day.

'Hi, what's up?' she messaged.

I didn't reply.

'I hope you remember me,' she typed.

WTF? How could anyone forget her? I wanted to say that to her, but didn't. I chose a simple 'Hi.. Ya, I do.'

'How are you?' she wrote.

'Fantastic.'

'Nice to hear that.' After a brief gap, 'I've read all your poems and posts. They're so nice.'

'Thanks,' I replied, adding a smiley at the end.

'I am happy that you even got an offer for a movie. Congratulations! Seems like you are on your way to something big,' she messaged.

I sent her a smiley again and added, 'I am doing my best and I hope everything turns out well.'

'It will,' she messaged and from there on our chatting sessions started.

We began talking about our good old schooldays, our classmates, and how life had treated us so far. I had barely been in touch with my schoolmates after that mishap during the match. Aditi was careful not to bring up that topic, for I think she knew I would feel sad.

So, instead, she asked me how my life had been after I left school. I told her only about the good things that had happened– getting into a good engineering college, a well-paying job at a reputed MNC, and writing lyrics.

She said that she had done a course in fashion designing from a top college in India and was looking forward to a career in fashion designing.

'*It will suit you,*' I messaged her.

'*Why do you think so?*'

I saw your pics and your dressing sense is absolutely amazing, I wanted to say, but I didn't. Instead I just typed, '*I don't know. I just felt so.*'

'*Achha.*'

After a while, she asked me, '*Where do you live in Bangalore?*'

'*BTM Layout.*'

'*Reallyyy????*'

'*Ya.*' I wondered why it astonished her so much.

'*Even I live in BTM Layout,*' she messaged.

'*Which phase?*'

'*2nd Main.*'

'*I live in 37th Main.*'

'*It is close by. I think we should catch up sometime,*' she said.

I can't tell you how many times I read that one line. All the while I was trying to put up a facade of not being too interested in the conversation so that I wouldn't look like one of those million guys after her. I was wondering how I would ask her out, but good heavens, when she herself said that we should meet, I felt quite ecstatic.

'*Sure,*' I gave her a one-word answer.

She was typing something, but before she could send it to me, I messaged her, '*Got to go now. Writing time.*'

She stopped typing and replied, '*Okay. Hope to see you soon.*'

'*Bye. Take care.*' I logged out.

I was actually dying to talk to her, but I deliberately stopped chatting with her. I tried to imagine myself in her shoes and I felt intuitively that my saying goodbye before her would actually put me in that 'different guy' zone. I felt I had seemed a cut above the rest by not showing much interest in her and I hoped she would fall for it. Also, I felt she would feel challenged to get my attention, now that she felt I was not just another guy drooling over her.

Girls like challenges, Krish had told me once. And their favourite challenge is to turn a guy who doesn't show interest in them into a guy who craves for them. I never really understood what kind of joy girls get in taming guys!

Over the next week, I didn't contact Aditi, even though I felt a strong urge to do so. Esha called me once and we did have steamy hot sex. I also had a good time with Ruchika after two days.

I met Anjali on a Friday evening in a restaurant and I told her about Aditi. Anjali made a face and told me that Aditi was a very selfish person. Anjali had been in touch with Aditi and she told me subtly that it would be wise to keep a distance from Aditi. I wondered if Anjali was feeling jealous, because I had never found Aditi selfish in any way. We didn't speak about Aditi anymore after that.

Next morning, at around eleven, I got a message from Aditi on Facebook. She said that she was at a McDonald's restaurant near my room and was waiting for a friend. I replied with an okay. She then started telling me that she had been waiting for her friend for an hour and her friend had not shown up. I again replied with a simple okay. She continued typing, bitching about how her friend never really stood by her word. I typed a simple '*Ha ha.. Happens*' and sent it to her. A brief silence ensued.

I was beginning to wonder if she was dropping a hint for me to meet her. I sensed that the friend who had ditched her was non-existent. And even though I wanted to ask her if I could meet her, I didn't. I held my horses and it paid off.

She sent me a message: '*What are you doing?*'

'*Just back from gym,*' I replied.

After a minute, she messaged: '*Hmm ... If you aren't busy with something, can we meet?*'

I pumped my fist in the air and mentally high-fived myself. I was going to meet Aditi, the most beautiful girl I had ever seen in my life. I was extremely excited that she had asked me to meet her.

I messaged her: '*Will be there in half an hour.*'

I took a steamy bath under the shower singing the song *Pehla Nasha* all the while. I then wore a nice T-shirt and a stylish jacket on top of it, and paired it off with faded jeans and canvas shoes. I then rushed to McDonald's on my bike.

When I went inside, I saw Aditi sitting demurely on a chair in a corner. She was typing something on her phone. I went near her and said, pointing to a chair opposite to her, 'Is this place already taken?'

'Ya, a friend is ...' She paused midway when she lifted her head and said, 'Heyy ... Hiiii!!' Excitement was writ large on her face.

Waving my hand, I said, 'Hi.' I wished I had extended my hand for a handshake, but I lacked the courage.

'Congratulations again, Mr Lyricist!' she said, extending her hand. I felt the same softness that I had felt when she had shaken my hand in school, after my match-winning performance. I wished I could hold her hand longer, but I pulled back after a while and sat across her.

'Let's order something. We can then sit and talk happily,' she said, flashing a pretty smile that could mellow down even the cruellest beast on the planet.

Like most girls I had met in my life, Aditi too liked talking a lot. I had almost mastered the art of listening and making people feel good about themselves, just by listening to them speaking their heart out. I tried doing that with Aditi too, but I couldn't; not because I wasn't interested in what she was saying, but because I was too distracted by her beauty.

While every other girl was getting her hair straightened, Aditi maintained lovely curly hair that went a little below her shoulders. The hair complemented her perfect oval-shaped face. Her hazel eyes had some magic in them and could entrap any guy. Her smile was to die for.

As she was talking, I was totally engrossed in the way she moved her lips, the way she blinked her eyes, and the way she tucked her hair behind her ears. But I did vaguely listen to what she was saying. She talked mostly about her days in college, about how she had lots of fun, and how badly she was missing it. I nodded my head once in a while, pretending to be listening to her.

After talking about her life vividly for more than half an hour, she smiled and said, 'I am sorry I kept on talking. Now you tell me what's up in your life?'

I didn't really want to answer her question as I now had to focus on talking and not looking at her. I couldn't tell her about Ruchika and Esha for obvious reasons, so I chose to talk about my passion for writing poems which had slowly given way to writing lyrics.

'You do write good lines,' she complimented me.

'Thank you.' I felt good.

'I remember one of your poems by heart. It is about how you feel when you love someone so much but you don't get back the same kind love from them,' she said and went on to recite what I had written. I was amazed because I myself had almost forgotten about it.

As she was reciting the lines, she got a call on her mobile. I slyly peeked to see who it was from and I was annoyed to see the name on display – 'Sweetheart'.

She excused herself saying she would be back in five minutes. I said okay even though I wasn't feeling okay.

Five minutes passed. Then ten, and then fifteen. There wasn't any sign of her returning. I was getting irritated. She came back after twenty minutes. Even before I said anything, she made an apologetic face and said, 'I am really really sorry.'

I feigned being normal and said, 'Your boyfriend?'

'Ya,' she said.

'Who is the lucky guy?'

'It's Siddharth. Our classmate.' She dropped a bomb.

I felt extreme frustration after she divulged the name. First, I was frustrated because she had a boyfriend. Second, because, of all the people in this world, she chose that fucking Siddharth. He hogged the limelight in school and now he hogged the heart of my crush. Man! It's so infuriating to know that your erstwhile arch-enemy is your crush's present boyfriend.

'What happened?' she asked, noticing the unpleasantness on my face.

'Does Siddharth know you met me?' I don't know why I asked her that question.

'Well, not really. He is kind of possessive and doesn't really like me meeting guys. Though he never puts any explicit restrictions, I can feel it,' she said, trying valiantly to hide something.

I tried being normal in vain, and just to say something, I asked, 'What is he doing now?'

'He runs a mobile application company and heads a team of forty people. He has even got funding from angel investors and spends most of his time working hard to make it big,' she said, proud of her super-smart successful boyfriend.

Listening to his accomplishments, I felt like a lowlife. I tried hard not to show my disappointment, but I couldn't really act well. I faked a smile, but I guess it was kind of evident that I wasn't happy with Aditi having a boyfriend.

I got up from my seat and said, without making eye contact, 'I need to go now. I have some work.'

She was surprised by my abruptness.

'Umm...okay,' she said, reluctantly.

I left without even saying goodbye and kicked a chair on my way out. And while I was returning home, I kept thinking to myself why I was feeling so annoyed. Aditi was beautiful and gorgeous and smart. I shouldn't have been so surprised to find out that she had a boyfriend. She would of course choose the best among the lot and Siddharth was indeed an amazing choice. For the first time in a long time, I felt like a loser.

I picked up a beer bottle on the way and headed for my place.

Once home, I opened my laptop and started writing. I realized that it wasn't Aditi having a boyfriend that was really bothering me. It was just that I wanted her to be mine, and not getting her would make me feel like a loser again. I had been a loser enough number of times in life, but ever since I had met Krish in Bangalore, I was on the path to getting whatever I wanted. Not having Aditi equated to not having what I wanted which equated to feeling like a loser again.

I called up Krish, but he disconnected. He was kind enough to send me a message on WhatsApp soon after, asking me what the matter was. I took a sip of beer and explained my predicament to him.

He sent a guffawing smiley and a WhatsApp forward. It read – 'Just because a goalpost has a goalkeeper, it doesn't mean you can't score goals.'

I smiled at his remark. His post was funny, yet true. But goalkeeper meant added difficulty.

I chatted with Krish for a while and then prepared to sleep. But just as I was about to hit bed, I got a notification of a friend request on Facebook. The profile had a picture of a Barbie doll and the name was quite silly, something like 'Beautiful Princess'. I didn't bother at all, for I felt it was just another fake profile. But then, as I was about to log out, I received a message.

'*Hey, it's Aditi,*' the message read.

It stunned me. I was confused and was wondering what to reply.

'*You left abruptly and I didn't really understand why. Sorry if I made you feel bad in any way,*' she messaged before I could reply. I checked her original profile and it was still there.

'*Why are you messaging from a fake profile?*' I asked to resolve my confusion.

'*It's that...*'

'*What's that?*'

'*Can you ignore that?*'

'*No, tell me,*' I insisted.

'*Well, I told you na ... Siddharth doesn't like me talking to other guys. It's just that I don't want him to know that we chat.*'

'*Ohh.*'

'*He knows the password of my Facebook account. He doesn't check though, but it's safer to use another profile,*' she revealed the secret.

I didn't know what to say. I sent a simple and safe message – 'Okay.'

'*Tell me, why did you leave abruptly?*' She brought back the question.

'*It's that...*'

'*What's that?*'

'*Can you ignore that?*'

'*No, tell me,*' she insisted this time.

'*Nothing. Really nothing,*' I lied.

I wondered why she was trying to put words in my mouth. Wasn't it obvious that I had left her because I couldn't digest that she was already in a relationship?

A brief silence ensued and she sent me a message soon after, '*I know you had a crush on me. Anjali already told me about that when we met.*'

Now it was my turn to be shocked. All the while I was pretending to be uninterested in her, but she already knew that I liked her immensely. Why did she pretend and act all the while? I guess I knew the answer – drama.

Girls love drama and Aditi proved to be no exception. Now that there was nothing I could say or do except tell her the truth, I messaged, '*Ya, I do have a crush on you and any guy would feel bad to find his crush with someone else.*' I was being honest, if nothing else.

'*I am sorry if you felt bad. I thought you would feel happy to see me,*' she said.

I took a sip of beer lying on the table and typed, '*I was … In fact, when I saw you for the first time in the restaurant, it was like … Like seeing a rainbow after the first rain … Like a cool breeze in hot summer … Like a snowflake in cold winter … And like the first leaves of spring.*' I didn't really know why I suddenly sent those lines.

'*Awww!*' she messaged followed by a smiley. I remained silent.

'*You could have stayed for some more time,*' she messaged.

I wanted to, but I felt bad. Staying would have made things worse. But I didn't tell her that. Instead I took another sip of beer and sent her another message:

Your curly hair entangle my thoughts,
Your hazel eyes hurl seductive darts.
Your smile seems like a fusion of arts,
And you have no idea how you crush a million hearts.

'*Oh my God!*' she messaged. '*So many people have complimented me, but none as creatively as you did. Thank you soooo much,*' she continued, the number of 'o's signifying that she was happy.

From there on, I started sending poems praising her beauty and she would feel ecstatic. Some of them were downright silly and some were moderately good. I was spinning the lines on the go and I wondered if she appreciated my effort more than the content of the poems.

As I was chatting, three points sprung up in my mind. One, she had a boyfriend and yet she wanted to talk to me secretly. Two, she already knew I had a crush on her. Three, she was actually feeling happy in my company. Connecting the three dots, it didn't take much time for me to realize that the goal could be scored. It was just that I needed to be a better striker and strike when the time was right!

We continued chatting till late in the night. But our chatting sessions didn't end that night. They continued every day. The only exception was when I spent time with Ruchika or Esha.

After a few days, Aditi asked if we could meet again. Why wouldn't I? I dressed in my best clothes again that day and went to a posh pub that Aditi had chosen.

When I went inside, Aditi was sitting as demurely as she had sat at McDonald's, but now with her head down. She was wearing a greenish-blue dress that reached just above her knees. I walked to her, sat on the chair across her and noticed a lovely necklace of white beads adorning her neck, a pair of matching earrings making her look ever so adorable.

She saw me and raised her head and I noticed a small teardrop trying to escape her eyes.

WTF? I said to myself. Aditi had everything that a girl could dream of – timeless beauty, a smart boyfriend, loads of cash, and a number of friends to party with. I wondered what would have made her sad.

But in an instant, I realized how wrong I was to think that pretty girls won't dwell in sadness. Everyone has their own story of misery, I felt.

She smiled widely, which I felt was quite unnecessary, and said hi. Her eyes weren't smiling by the way. I smiled in return and asked her formally, 'How are you?'

'I am fine,' she said, continuing her fake smile.

'I am fine' is the most popular lie ever told, I guess!

I wanted to ask her why she was sad, but I sensed that she would divulge anyway and so I didn't really push her much. I felt that the very reason she had asked to meet me was to share her sadness. So I waited.

The waiter came to us to take our order. 'Screwdriver,' she said and I ordered a beer for myself. Aditi's order didn't surprise me much, for she was a party girl and alcohol was quite common in the kind of parties she went to.

We started talking while waiting for our drinks. We spoke about the latest music and movies. Most of our talk was about trivia that one could live without.

When the waiter brought the drinks, Aditi finished the entire drink in one shot. She squinted her eyes as the drink slid down her throat. Her eyes turned slightly red, but to my surprise, she looked at the waiter and said, 'Bring two more.'

I took a sip of beer and began observing her. It didn't take a genius to understand that she was trying to drown her sadness in vodka. And one glass down, she began opening up. 'You know, I love him like crazy. But I don't think he loves me as much as I love him.'

She was obviously talking about Siddharth. Though I felt a twinge of jealousy, I kept calm and mumbled, 'Hmm.'

'He wasn't like this before. He used to call me every day, buy me many gifts, and die to meet me even if it was only for a little while. It's only after he started that stupid company, that he never finds the time for me. He doesn't take my calls and calls back only when he feels like. I feel so ignored, Arjun.' Aditi began sobbing.

I didn't know what to say or do. I wanted to wipe her tears, not really to console her, but to milk the opportunity to touch her cheeks. But I didn't do so as Aditi and I were yet to grow comfortable with each other. It was only our second meeting. So I offered her a tissue instead.

She wiped her tears saying thanks, but the tears didn't stop. Meanwhile, the waiter brought her another drink. And again, Aditi drank it bottoms up. She closed her eyes and took a deep breath, as if trying to push the tears back into her eyes.

She opened her eyes after a while and shook her head again, this time more so because of the high she experienced. And as the DJ started playing the music, she held my hand and pulled me to the dance floor.

I looked at Aditi in wonder. She was dancing like there was no tomorrow. The alcohol was probably getting the better of her as she did some raunchy moves. She moved her body according to the rhythm of the music and I tried hard to keep up with her.

But after some time, she did the unthinkable. She took my hands and put them on her waist and smiled naughtily. I was stunned, while she continued dancing. I tried to mimic the moves that didn't seem feminine, but it was my hands that were having a feast, touching her waist over the smooth fabric. I was enjoying the moment.

But it wasn't to last. Aditi slipped and fell on the floor, spraining her ankle in the process. I helped her up and made her sit on a chair. I took an ice cube and began applying it to the sprain. Her feet were as soft as her hands and as I applied the ice holding her leg in my hand, I saw Aditi's eyes were teary again. I don't know why but I felt that she was overwhelmed by the care I was taking of her. Or maybe it reminded her of how Siddharth used to take care of her!

Later, I dropped her home and headed back to my room. Along the way, I realized how much of an asshole I had become. When Aditi was crying, I had wanted to touch her cheeks. When she sprained her ankle, I was more than happy to hold her feet and ogle her waxed legs.

Lust is the strongest feeling – whoever said that hadn't lied!

■

After that day, Aditi and I began meeting quite often, almost every alternate day. The venue was always decided by her and it was usually some pub or the other. She paid the bill almost always. Though meeting her didn't burn a hole in my pocket, her occasional sobbing about Siddharth did burn a hole in my heart.

On one such occasion, when Aditi was sobbing about Sid's lack of interest in her, I wiped her tears with my hand. She didn't mind. I then pulled her cheeks and said something I felt was very clichéd, but it worked. I said, 'You look beautiful even when you are sad.' She smiled and thanked me. After that, physical touch between us wasn't an issue at all. She never stopped me from holding her hands, putting my hands around her shoulders, or brushing away her hair from her face. I wanted to take it further, but was just waiting for the right moment, which came sooner than I had expected.

During one of our late-night chats, I was praising Aditi, saying how sweet she always looked. Instead of thanking me for my compliments, like she usually did, she messaged, *Just sweet??*'

'Yes, very sweet,' I said, without thinking much.

'Hmm.'

She went offline for a while, which left me confused. After some time, she sent me a pic with her fluffy dog. 'Me with my sweet Toffee' was the caption of the pic. Obviously, Toffee was the dog's name. It was indeed cute and the adjective sweet was apt for it. But it wasn't the dog that caught my attention. I observed the pic closely and saw

Aditi was wearing *only* a loose shirt and nothing else. Her legs in the pic were slightly blurred, but that didn't stop her from looking extremely hot and I couldn't stop myself from getting a hard-on in my pants, looking at her smooth, milky thighs.

'*What happened? You okay?*' she messaged as I was so lost in looking at her that I even forgot to reply.

You look hot, I wanted to reply. But I sent: '*You are crazy!*'

'*I know,*' she said, with a lot of smileys at the end.

'*What's the craziest thing you have done?*'

'*Well ...*' I said, wondering for a while if I should tell her about the crazy game that I had played with Esha. After deliberating for a while, I took a chance and told her everything in detail. Sharing secrets does bring two people closer, I felt. And it worked.

Aditi messaged, after reading the whole thing I had sent: '*That indeed seems interesting and somewhat crazy.*'

'*What's the craziest thing you have done?*' I asked her.

'*Lots actually!!!*' pat came the reply.

'*One sample please,*' I messaged, wondering what she might have done. Aditi seemed like a sweet girl, not the crazy types.

'*What are your plans for new year?*' she messaged, without answering my question.

'*Haven't planned anything yet,*' I said.

'*Don't make any plans,*' she messaged and then said bye. I was confused.

■

A week later, just before New Year's Eve, Aditi messaged me to get ready by 11 p.m. the next day. She said that she would pick me up from home and we would head to a party. I asked her for more details, but she didn't divulge.

As I was getting ready for the event, I got a call from Anjali. I was in an ecstatic mood then, eager to spend time with Aditi, and so I didn't take the call. I simply sent her an sms, forwarding one of those quick message templates – 'I am busy right now. Call you later.' But she replied, 'Please call me as soon as possible. It's urgent.'

It was unusual for Anjali to ask me to call her back urgently, for she always waited till I called back. I sensed something was wrong, but as I was about to dial her number, I got a message from Aditi saying she would be coming to my room in a few minutes. I chucked the idea of calling Anjali and began getting ready hurriedly.

Aditi came to my room at 11 p.m. sharp. Like I always did when I went out with Aditi, I dressed my best, this time wearing funky party wear. When I went downstairs, I saw Aditi sitting in a luxury Audi car. I knew she was quite rich, but I didn't know she drove an Audi too.

I opened the door and sat in the front seat. I turned my head to see Aditi and what a sight it was! She was wearing a black dress decorated with sequins. It was a round-neck, sleeveless dress and was transparent till her breasts. It barely covered her thighs and the black dress on her fair skin made her look even more ravishing than usual.

We said hi to each other and before I could start talking, she raced the car. I wanted to ask her where she was going to take me, but I decided not to.

As she was driving, I couldn't help but admire her super smooth waxed legs. I was dying to move my fingers down her thighs and then upwards. But I refrained, though with much difficulty.

After about half an hour, we reached the outskirts of Bangalore. The road was lined with trees on both sides and it was pitch-dark. Except for a few vehicles now and then, it was mostly deserted. Even though I didn't feel like asking, my curiosity got the better of me and I asked her, 'Where are we going?'

'To a party,' she stated the obvious.

'I know that,' I said. 'Is there any pub which is so far from the main city?'

'We aren't going to a pub or anything,' she said, rocking her head to the music playing in the car.

'Then?'

'You wanted to know the crazy side of me, right? You'll see that today,' she said.

I was still confused and wasn't sure what was running in her mind.

After driving for fifteen more minutes, Aditi took a sharp left turn. I was startled as she drove rashly on a muddy road which seemed like a driveway straight out of horror movies. A few minutes later, a huge black gate appeared. She honked and two watchmen asked her for some pass. She showed it to them and they let us in. There were about forty luxury cars in the parking lot. I was slowly beginning to understand where she had brought me.

She parked the car along with the other cars, checked herself in the mirror for a while and then we both got down. She came towards me, held my hand, and led me. I followed her without asking any questions.

As we walked along the path, I could hear the music. It didn't take me much time to realize that it was a farmhouse and a bunch of rich kids had decided to celebrate New Year there. I was right this time, except that the party was way different from any kind of party I had ever seen in my life.

As the path curved beyond the house, I saw sixty–seventy young boys and girls dancing disjointedly to groovy sound beats being played by an enthusiastic DJ. It was a pool party; most girls were dressed scantily and the guys were in shorts. Bottles and glasses of alcohol were lined up alongside the pool.

Some people were dancing in the water, others were lying by the pool, and there were couples kissing each other and playing with each other's bodies. Some relatively sane ones were tapping their feet a little away from the pool.

I had only heard of such parties, but it was the first time in my life that I was witnessing one. I tried being normal, for I didn't want Aditi to think that I was entirely new to this culture. I might appear uncool, I felt. But I think my expressions were a dead giveaway and Aditi knew that I was surprised.

As we joined the group, she introduced me to a friend of hers. The guy was wearing a loose sleeveless shirt and three-fourth pants. He looked like a rapper, with the tattoos on his shoulders and a hip-hop cap. He spoke with a heavy accent and after a while he smiled when Aditi whispered something in his ear.

He went inside a tiny room and came back with a syringe filled with some liquid. He also brought a pill. Aditi took them from him and they high-fived each other.

She gave me the pill and asked me to swallow it.

'What's this?' I asked.

'You ask too many questions. Just have it. You'll feel good,' she said, as she transferred the fluid from the syringe into her veins.

I watched her in surprise and took the pill. It didn't have any immediate effect on me, but I saw Aditi slowly transforming from a super-sweet person into a maniac.

'What did you take?' I asked, more out of curiosity than concern.

'Coke,' she said.

'I didn't know that a cold drink can be taken in the veins,' I said innocently.

She guffawed at my answer and said, 'Coke is short for cocaine.'

I then realized it wasn't just a pool party, but a *rave party*. I turned around and observed people around me. Everyone was high. There was euphoria all around and people were having the time of their lives. But more than them, it was Aditi who caught my attention.

She began looking at me dreamily, her eyes almost inside her head. She let her hair down and began rocking to the music. Her body swayed as she danced and her moves were incredibly sexy.

She held my hand and urged me to dance. I shed my inhibitions and moved my body.

As time passed, the pill began to have its effect on me. I was filled with a strange kind of ecstasy. It was an out-of-the-world feeling and I felt a sudden burst of extreme happiness inside me. I would know later that the pill that I had taken was itself called ecstasy!

After dancing for a while, Aditi excused herself and came back with another shot of coke. I warned her, but she didn't pay any heed.

'Fuck this world. Fuck everyone,' she said as she shot the coke blood through her veins. After that shot, Aditi went wild and it became extremely difficult for me to control her. She began dancing crazily like there was no tomorrow, her hands moving in the air, her legs barely supporting her raving body.

As if the frenzied dancing was not enough, Aditi started dancing seductively. She held my hands and put them on her waist, like she had done in the pub.

'You always wanted to hold me, right?' Aditi said, looking at me seductively with her hazel eyes. It meant that she knew of my intentions and it reinforced my belief that girls sense a guy's intentions easily, but just feign innocence.

Now that the cat was out of the bag, I told her that I had many wet dreams thinking about her. She grinned from ear to ear and pulled my nose saying, 'Naughty boy.' She then put her arms around my neck and moved her body closer to me. I tried to keep a distance, lest she feel the hard-on in my pants. But in spite of my trying, Aditi pulled me closer and I was almost hugging her, the erection in my pants now touching her body.

We looked at each other. I guess it was inevitable that our lips met.

I had kissed before, but I can tell you without any doubt that kissing your first crush is an entirely different feeling. Maybe it's because your first crush is the first person who introduced sexual ecstasy in your life, although through fantasies. And seeing a fantasy coming true is in itself an amazing feeling.

I don't know for how long we kissed each other. All I know was I didn't want to stop. The strawberry flavour of her lip balm made the kiss even more delicious. We had to stop because it had become difficult to breathe. I looked around and no one was really bothered about us. Most of them were too involved in their own affairs.

Aditi saw the hunger in my eyes. She held my hand, like she always did, and pulled me away from the crowd. We walked quickly along a narrow path in a manicured lawn, away from the party scene. Soon, we ended up alone in the garden.

No sooner had we placed ourselves behind the trunk of a huge tree than Aditi began kissing me hungrily. I kissed her back with equal fervour, entangling my fingers in her curly hair. She put her hand behind my neck and pulled me closer. I closed my eyes in elation and opened them after a while. Aditi looked extremely beautiful in the moonlight. The stars filled the sky above and crickets were chirping in the background as we began making love.

I moved my hands slowly towards Aditi's back and unzipped her dress. Gravity did its job well as her dress fell off her smooth body. Aditi removed my T-shirt and unbuckled my belt in a jiffy. She pulled my pants down and saw my manhood which desperately wanted to be freed.

I smiled mischievously as I watched Aditi looking coy. She was in her undergarments – black and semi-transparent. She looked like a sexy Kingfisher model.

I didn't want to waste time and began kissing Aditi again. I moved from her strawberry-flavoured lips to her cheeks to her ears and to her neck and then towards her super smooth taut breasts. The bra had a simple hook in the front and, thank heavens, it was easier to remove. I twirled my tongue around her hardened nipple as she sighed in ecstasy. I fondled the other breast which felt like a marshmallow.

We then freed ourselves of our remaining clothes and lay on the ground. The grass was cold, but our bodies were hot, burning with desire. And under the moonlit sky, as millions of stars watched us, Aditi and I made love. I played with her body and she moaned and heaved and sighed and groaned, and the sounds felt like music to my ears.

Thanks to Krish's safety packets in my wallet, I entered her, wearing a helmet on my shaft. I had had sex before, but it didn't come close to what I was feeling now. I think the drugs had made our bodies supersensitive to touch and the hormones were overflowing, giving inexplicable pleasure, taking us to a virtual paradise.

Aditi rolled me over and began riding me. I closed my eyes dreamily and felt her on me. And then, Aditi's phone began to ring. I was sure that she wouldn't take the call, but to my surprise, she did. And it was from none other than that stupid Siddharth!

She spoke to him, while she continued riding me. She told him that she was at a party with a friend. So technically, she wasn't even lying. She wished him Happy New Year and disconnected the call. I felt a little weird, but at the same time I felt like I had taken revenge on Siddharth for all the times he had caused me pain, fucking his girlfriend while he was talking with her on the phone.

After fucking our brains out, Aditi and I lay naked on the grass, with her head resting on my arm. The moon hid behind the clouds and the environment around us turned dark.

Rahul

I woke up the next morning in my room, trying to recollect the shenanigans of the previous night. I couldn't remember how I had ended up in my room. It was 1 p.m. and there were five missed calls on my phone – all of them from Anjali. I called her back soon after, only to hear both panic and relief in her voice.

'Everything okay?' I asked her.

'It's okay *now*. But it wasn't last night,' she said.

'What happened?'

'Dad had a massive heart attack.'

'Whaaaat?' I jumped from my bed.

'Yeah, I was in the ambulance when I called you last night,' she said.

As soon as I heard that, I began feeling guilty. All my life, Anjali had always been there every time I needed any help. She had been my strongest pillar of support. But when she had needed my help, at the most crucial time, I wasn't there for her. I should have at least called her back, I told myself.

Breaking my train of thought, Anjali said, 'If it wasn't for Rahul, my dad would've stopped breathing by now.'

'Rahul?' I asked, out of curiosity.

'Yes, Rahul. Remember the guy I told you about when we first met in Hyderabad? My senior.'

'Oh...I guess I do,' I said, trying to recollect what she had said about him.

'So what really happened?' I asked Anjali, more out of obligation.

She said in a monotone, 'I had to stay late in college yesterday and Rahul dropped me home. Dad opened the door and welcomed both of us warmly. But within a few minutes, he began sweating profusely and his face contorted. He stumbled a bit and collapsed on the floor. Rahul was quick to respond and, before things became worse, he performed CPR on him.'

'Oh.'

'I was panicking and lost my mind completely. Rahul's reassuring words calmed me as I made a call to the ambulance. And by the time the ambulance arrived, thanks to Rahul, Dad had started breathing again.'

'Oh.'

'He stayed by Dad in the ambulance and made frantic calls to the doctors in the hospital to make arrangements by the time we reached there. Even after we reached the hospital, Rahul was by Dad's side as his fellow doctors gave him medication. Any delay would have cost him his life,' she ended with a sigh of relief.

'It's good to hear that your dad is out of danger,' I said.

'Yeah. I had my heart in my mouth the whole night. I dread to think what could have happened if Rahul wasn't by my side,' she said.

'Even I feel like thanking him,' I said.

'You should meet him sometime. He is a very nice guy,' she said.

'Let's plan,' I said as my phone went off because of low battery. I didn't bother to call Anjali again as my head felt heavy and I was craving to go back to sleep. Deep inside, I was glad that Anjali hadn't felt bad that I had missed her call when she really needed me. The guilt vanished and I went back to being normal again.

Late in the evening, Aditi came to my room and we had another hot session in bed. I enjoyed every bit of it and the best part was that there was more to come.

Aditi would come to my place once in a while and we would have a good time together. She had a boyfriend and yet she would have romance with me. Initially, I felt somewhat guilty and the entire thing felt unethical. But I justified my actions by telling myself that ethics and values are only for losers. And moreover, it wasn't my problem anyway. It was Aditi's. She felt good in my company and that's what mattered. Whenever she came to my room, along with pleasure, she brought cocaine and weed, every single time.

For some reason, I preferred weed to cocaine as it gave me a different kind of happiness, not just to my body, but also to my soul. I became addicted to it and not a day went by without my smoking a joint. For some incomprehensible reason, I became more creative after smoking weed. Words flowed smoothly from my pen and lyrics composed after weed came out more beautifully. When I submitted the lyrics of the six songs to the director who had offered me the movie, he was more than ecstatic. Even the music director was so impressed that he promised to recommend me for his next movie. Things were going in the right direction and I felt good.

■

During one of the smoke breaks at office, I told Krish about my conquests and told him proudly how I had nailed Aditi, after Ruchika and Esha. He smiled philosophically and wished me all the best for my future adventures. I wanted to thank him, but unlike girls, guys don't thank their guy friends verbally. It just doesn't seem right. So instead of thanking him, I told him to ask me for any help, if he ever needed anything. He smiled again silently, lit a cigarette, and changed the topic.

What was it with Krish? Why did he behave oddly sometimes?

■

One Friday evening, Anjali called me. After talking for some time about her dad's health, she asked me if I was free the next day to watch a movie with her. I wasn't really interested, but she rarely asked me for anything, so I couldn't say no to her.

'Book three tickets instead of two,' she said to someone.

'Three?'

'Yeah, Rahul is also coming.'

'Oh. Okay,' I said.

We spoke casually for a little while. I couldn't tell her about Aditi obviously, but I did tell her about the positive response from the music director and a possible offer for another movie. Anjali was quite happy to hear the news.

After I was done, she told me about a cultural fest that had happened in her college recently. Rahul and Anjali had danced to a duet and they had won the first prize for their ball dance. I teased her playfully asking if they were the only ones who participated in the event and she showed some mock anger.

She hung up soon after.

The next day, Anjali came to my room and picked me up. We went to the Forum mall in her car.

We went inside the mall and waited for Rahul. The show was about to begin and Anjali was fretting as she didn't want to miss the beginning.

'Why is he taking so much...' Anjali said, 'Ah, here he comes.'

I turned my head towards the guy Anjali was looking at. He was tall, fair, and handsome, and with side-parted silky hair, he indeed looked like Shah Rukh Khan in his younger days.

He was wearing a white round-neck t-shirt with a sexy brown jacket. His blue jeans and Ferrari shoes made the look complete. As he was walking towards us, he removed his branded sunglasses and tucked them in his T-shirt. His gait was stylish and I must say he looked very charming.

'Idiot, why so late?' Anjali asked him, while she mock-punched him on his arm.

'Ouch,' he feigned pain. He put his hand inside the pocket of the jacket and took out a small box of Ferrero Rocher chocolates.

'Late because of this,' he said, showing the chocolates in his hand.

'So sweet,' Anjali said and pulled his cheeks.

She took the chocolates from Rahul and gave one to me, 'By the way, Rahul, this is Arjun. And Arjun, this is Rahul.' It was just a formality.

'Hi,' Rahul and I said at the same time and shook hands.

'Chalo, the movie is about to begin.' Anjali made us rush inside the theatre.

We occupied our seats as the 'No smoking' ads came on the screen. Anjali was happy that the movie hadn't started. She sat between Rahul and me.

The movie began and, in no time, Anjali began talking to me. Parts of the movie were shot in Anjali's college and she kept telling me about it. Being a lyricist, I was interested mostly in the lyrics of the songs and I didn't really mind Anjali talking to me all the while.

I observed Rahul sometimes when I had to turn to listen to Anjali. He was enjoying the movie quietly. I thought he would feel left out if he wasn't involved in the conversation, but he didn't seem to mind at all. He was cool in his own skin.

The scene just before the interval was shot right in front of Anjali's classroom and Anjali was there in the background. Excitement was quite evident on Anjali's face, and during the interval, she began narrating everything that had happened the day the scene was shot.

I got up to bring popcorn and Coke for the three of us. But Anjali held my hand and made me sit. She turned to Rahul and asked him to get some popcorn. Rahul obliged without saying anything and Anjali continued her story. I was listening to her, but at the same time, I wondered how Rahul must have felt. But when he came back with the popcorn, there wasn't any expression on his face that showed any kind of dejection. He smiled pleasantly when he gave us our buckets and took his seat.

The movie ended eventually and, more than listening to the dialogues of the hero and the heroine, I had listened to Anjali.

We came out from the theatre and Anjali headed towards the washroom saying she would be back in a moment. Rahul and I waited for her outside a women's clothing shop, albeit a few steps away.

'So you enjoyed the movie?' Rahul initiated the conversation. He was smiling.

'Ya, the movie was good,' I said, sighing.

I think sarcasm comes naturally to guys.

'I hope Anjali didn't bore you with her continuous talking. She does talk a lot when she is excited about something,' Rahul said.

I smiled and he continued, 'She tells me a lot about you too. Arjun this. Arjun that. And the thing is – she never gets bored of talking about you.'

'Really?' I said and chuckled.

'Ya, man,' Rahul said.

'I am really sorry for the trouble, dude,' I said.

'That's okay, man. Don't worry. You don't have to be sorry. I never get irritated with Anjali anyway, no matter what she says or what she does. It's like ...'

He stopped midway and turned to his right. He began looking at Anjali who was walking towards us. In the light-blue kurti and white leggings, topped with a long, white transparent chunni that almost touched the floor, Anjali was looking prettier than the beautiful mannequin behind her. Her walking style was elegant and she oozed class.

I don't know why but at that moment I noticed Rahul and he was marvelling at Anjali's beauty. His mouth was wide open and his eyes were shining bright – a dead giveaway that he liked Anjali a lot. He was totally captivated by her beauty.

As Anjali neared us, she became a bit conscious. She checked her dress once and said, 'Anything wrong?'

I think even the world's prettiest girl needs assurance and validation from men that she is pretty. Anjali was no exception, I guessed, for she could have easily figured out that Rahul was bowled over by her beauty.

'We were actually looking at...the mannequin behind you,' I said.

Anjali hit me on my arm and said, 'Idiot!'

'Chalo, let's go downstairs,' Anjali said and we walked towards the slow-moving escalator, with Rahul beside her and me trailing behind.

No sooner had we stepped on the escalator than Anjali shrieked in pain. She stumbled and fell down. Before I realized what had happened, both ends of Anjali's chunni were stuck between the steps and the sidebar. But within a nanosecond, Rahul held Anjali's chunni tightly, else God only knows what would have happened to her. The chunni got torn but Anjali was safe. Shock and horror was writ all over her face and she began sobbing uncontrollably.

Rahul was equally worried. He put his arm around her and made her sit on a comfortable sofa nearby. He then rushed to a nearby counter and bought a bottle of water.

As Anjali drank the water, he caressed her head slowly, in an attempt to relieve her from shock.

I sat beside Anjali and didn't really do anything. I took a backseat as Rahul was anyway taking care of her.

Anjali was still crying. Rahul wiped the tears from her face. He held her face with both his hands and said, 'Everything is okay. Don't worry. I am here. Everything is okay.'

While he was saying this, Anjali held my hand tightly. Her palms were sweaty, maybe because of the sudden shock. Rahul was too busy looking at Anjali to notice her hand in mine. All I did was put my hand on hers.

After a few moments, Anjali took her hand away from mine and wiped her tears. Rahul sat on the other side. He was still pacifying her, soothing her, and trying his best to calm her down.

Anjali regained composure after some time and we decided to leave. We chose the lift instead of the escalator this time.

Rahul had to leave as he needed to join duty at the hospital. But before leaving, he did make sure that Anjali was okay. Only after Anjali told him repeatedly that she was fine did he leave us.

While heading towards the parking lot, I asked Anjali if I should drive the car. Anjali refused, saying she was okay now. I didn't have any problem with that.

We reached my room and Anjali came upstairs. The room was disorganized and Anjali sighed as soon as she saw it. But she patiently put things in their respective places, arranged my cupboard properly, and then sat on the beanbag. I sat on the bed and she began talking.

For the first time since I had come to Bangalore, Anjali spoke at length about Rahul. She kept singing praises about him. She kept telling me what a nice guy he was, how caring he had always been, how he had guided her during the medicine course, and encouraged her every time her morale was low. She told me about many instances when Rahul had steered her out of problems. Once when she lost her record just before the practical exam, it was Rahul who stayed awake the whole night and finished writing it in time. Another time, when Anjali was being harassed by one of the college professors, it was Rahul who spoke to the dean without fear and made sure the professor was taken to task. Also, every time Anjali had any doubt regarding anything, it was Rahul who would become her Google and answer all her questions.

Not just in academics, Rahul supported Anjali in every matter of her life. He stayed by her side through all the good times and bad. He listened to her patiently, no matter how long she kept blabbering about silly things in her life. He advised her about things as trivial as what to wear for the farewell party to something as important as how to shape her career as a doctor. In short, he was to Anjali what Anjali was to me. And from what I heard about him from Anjali, I felt that he was indeed a gem of a person and whoever married him was going to be a very lucky girl.

Anjali continued speaking about him for an hour or so and then fell silent all of sudden.

After listening to her patiently all the while, I said, 'Anjali.'

'What?'

'He loves you a lot.'

'Hmm. You really think so?'

'I am pretty sure. I read his eyes while he was looking at you in the mall. They were filled with love and admiration.' Being a lyricist, I couldn't help being a little poetic.

Anjali didn't say anything. She looked into my eyes intently and fell silent for one whole minute. I couldn't guess what was going on in her mind.

She came and sat beside me. Resting her head on my shoulder, she snuggled her arm around mine and held my hand. I didn't move and we were silent. She then took my hand and put it on her cheek.

'I wish someone could read my eyes too,' she said and sighed.

'Hmm.'

■

After I spent Saturday with Anjali and Rahul, more out of obligation than anything else, I spent the whole of Sunday with Esha at her place. It was a perfect way to spend the day.

All in all, life was going great. I was now juggling between Ruchika, Esha, and Aditi, and I felt like I had become a playboy. Each one of them was like an ice-cream flavour to me. They all tasted different and yet every flavour was quite enjoyable.

Being at such a phase in life boosted my ego significantly and felt on top of the world. It was one of those times when everything goes in your favour. Everything you touch becomes gold. I wasn't sure how long it would last, so I decided to make the most of it. More than feeling like a winner now, I was happy that I didn't consider myself a loser anymore.

But then, just when I was thinking that life was at its best, I didn't know that something much better was yet to come along. Yes, when it rains, it pours!

■

After one of our sessions in bed, Ruchika told me that she was going to get married in two weeks and it was going to be the last time we would meet. Her parents had selected a rich, good-looking, and smart guy who was settled in the US and she didn't find any reason to say no to them.

Quite frankly, I was perfectly okay with that. I had had my time with Ruchika and our relationship was at the brink of falling apart, as we were almost bored with each other. If it weren't for the raging hormones, we would have fallen apart much earlier.

We kissed for probably the last time and wished each other good luck. I wasn't sad or anything, but I knew that I would never

ever forget Ruchika, for I lost my virginity to her. First things are always special, even long after they fade away!

I attended Ruchika's lavish wedding after two weeks along with my colleagues. While everybody else saw her in bridal wear, with jewellery and make-up, in my mind's eye, I saw her naked. In a way, it was funny and I was smiling to myself. Krish saw it and our eyes met. I think he understood what I was thinking.

Anyway, I went on the stage and congratulated the couple. I posed for a photograph and when I told Ruchika's husband that he was lucky, I really meant it. I smiled at Ruchika and she smiled back – a smile the meaning of which was known only to her and me. I said goodbye to her, knowing I wouldn't meet her in a very long time.

I came back to my room, thinking about Ruchika.

She had loved someone before she met me. After the break-up, she lusted for me. Now, she was getting married to another guy. As I continued thinking, it dawned upon me slowly that Love, Lust, and Marriage are actually three different sets. And sometimes, the intersection between the three can be a null set.

Moreover, I didn't find fault with Ruchika in any way. 'Ethics and values' are a foreign language to the heart and the heart just never understands it. It just wants what it wants. We live only once. So why not have fun during the short stint on this planet instead of living a life of compromise and misery?

■

There are two kinds of good-looking women in India. Those who look beautiful when they wear a sari, and those who make the sari look beautiful when they wear it. Smita was of the second kind. She had replaced Ruchika next to me in office.

She had a perfectly round face which was always adorned by a tiny, perfectly round bindi. She always wore cotton or georgette saris with short-sleeved blouses.

She had a pleasant face and a beatific smile too, but it wasn't Smita's lovely face or elegance that attracted me to her. It was her seductive gait that got me completely. The way her hips swayed when she walked was incredibly sexy.

Since Smita and I had to work together on the same project, we spent an awful lot of time together and inevitably became closer to each other. One thing led to another, and even though she was married with two kids, I ended up having an affair with her. A part of my soul did feel it was wrong, but my ego strangulated it. All I cared about was pleasure. And strangely, I realized that something that's forbidden is what gives a kick.

Smita had been married for seven years and she confessed during one of our lovemaking sessions that her life had come to a standstill, taken over by routine. The spark had gone, there were no more surprises, and happiness was now replaced with compromise. Her affair with me had brought back some excitement in her otherwise dull life. I was, for her, like a fresh spring after a dry winter. Or at least I thought so.

■

Ruchika, Esha, Aditi, and Smita – I had had four women since I landed in Bangalore. But my luck didn't stop there. As if four women were not enough, I ended up having an affair with another girl – Preeti – the granddaughter of the owners of my penthouse.

She was just eighteen years old and she apparently got attracted when she saw me doing push-ups, wearing nothing but shorts. My muscles had grown and were carved at the right places. The girl was too young to resist falling for a guy with a chiselled body, thanks to her overexposure to mainstream and social media. And I took advantage of it.

It wouldn't be correct to say that I made her fall in love with me. Rather, saying that I trapped her would be more appropriate. I played with her emotions, manipulated her feelings, and changed her thoughts. Since seduction now came naturally to me, I took her to bed within two weeks of meeting her. We had sex right under the nose of her grandparents, figuratively, but literally above their heads, on the first floor, and they remained oblivious of her mischiefs.

Preeti was like a bud and it was a different experience to be the guy who broke her cherry. But then, inevitably, she became very clingy and possessive. She did a lot of drama too. So it was a source of great relief for me that she lived in a hostel in the outskirts and came home only once in a while. Her constant nagging on the phone was pleasingly irritating and yet slightly inconvenient – something I could live with.

■

Meanwhile, the music director called me to meet a producer and the deal for a new movie was almost finalized. I felt happy, and I don't know why, but a flurry of sad thoughts filled my mind soon after and I began thinking about my mom and dad.

They wouldn't have been proud to see their son turning into a flirt and sleeping with multiple women, but I wished I could talk to them just once to tell them how their son had now become a lyricist. I wished they could see my name when it came rolling in the credits. I am sure it would have made them happy.

That evening I called Anjali soon after I left the office. She had some important things to do, but from my voice she sensed that I wasn't really okay. So she made time and met me.

As soon as she saw me, she asked me what was wrong and if she could help me in any way. I didn't reply and instead asked her if we could go to a movie. She readily obliged, like she always did, and we went to some senseless Bollywood movie that wouldn't consume much brain space. After that we had dinner together.

All the while, I barely said anything. But when I came back to my room after dropping her, I felt better. That's the magic of friendship. You don't really need to talk to your best friends to make yourself feel better. Just spending some time with them in silence is more than enough.

'*You're the sweetest person in this world,*' I messaged Anjali before going to sleep.

':)' she replied.

■

On a Friday evening, soon after I reached my room, I switched off my phone and began writing about my shenanigans since I had come to Bangalore. I couldn't believe that it was me who had done all those nasty things. I wondered what had made me the person I had become.

Obviously, I had been fed up with being a nice guy and ending up as a loser. My ego had taken a violent beating. I had needed to prove to myself that I was not a loser and I could get girls too. Luckily, Krish came into my life and made me understand women better. And now, here I was, from being a guy who had never kissed a girl before to a sex god who nailed five women in just nine months. The feeling was quite overwhelming and I was on top of the world.

I met Krish and told him how I felt. I owed him so much that I couldn't repay, no matter what.

Krish listened to me and said that he was happy for me, but I felt it lacked warmth. He told me to make hay while the sun shines. Feelings, emotions, and opinions change as time passes, he concluded. I listened to those words, but I didn't take them seriously. I was more interested in enjoying the erotic moments in my life.

But then...

The void

It had been a year since I left Hyderabad for Bangalore. So many changes had taken place in a relatively short period of time. I was at a high point in life as everything was coming my way.

The movie for which I had written lyrics was about to release and the offer to write lyrics for a reputed production house was confirmed. I had been promoted recently with a forty percent hike in my salary. I had made good friends in office and my social circle was brimming with lots of interesting people. Thanks to my dedication at the gym, I had become quite muscular and a hunk. There were enough female fans on Facebook, both for my looks and for my lyrics. I had also slept with a fairly good number of women and the experience had been quite thrilling. To top it all, I had been blessed with friends like Krish and Anjali who were always there by my side, whenever I needed them.

But, in spite of all this, for the past one month I had been suffering from a strange kind of void in my life. I had everything I wanted, but I wasn't really happy. Something was missing – some crucial piece of the puzzle. I couldn't figure out, no matter how hard I tried.

Thoughts of this void overwhelmed me. I tried to find an escape, dodging the desolation by having wild sex or smoking good amounts of weed. But they provided only temporary relief. The emptiness would resurface time and again, and I was clueless about how to overcome it. I racked my brain on many sleepless nights and yet found myself back to square one. It was extremely frustrating. The more I tried to solve my problem, the more futile it seemed. Moreover, the problem could be solved only if I knew what the problem was! Not knowing what my problem actually was, was in itself a big problem.

I even tried seeing a therapist, but in vain. And after spending a lot of time, thinking about my annoying thoughts, I just let time find out the answers for me. I let go and began learning to live with the emptiness. And boy, time didn't disappoint me. Not one bit!

■

One Saturday morning, for probably the first time in months, I didn't feel like going to the gym. Instead, I slumped on my beanbag, thinking about my parents. It was exactly a year since the bomb blast had taken away the two dearest people in my life.

No matter how great you become and no matter how much happiness you experience, all that seems incomplete when not shared with your loved ones. I had kept myself very busy so as not to miss my parents, but they were always there at the back of my mind. On their first death anniversary, I missed them more than ever. I badly wished they were by my side. I would have proudly taken them to the screening of my debut movie as a lyricist. But it would never happen. Never!

Before the thoughts crippled me, pushing me into emptiness again, I tried to regain my composure by lighting a joint. It didn't have much effect. So I thought of calling Ruchika just to talk to her for a while. I wondered if she missed me. I called her and she picked up the phone, but she promptly said that she was with her husband and would call me sometime later. Okay was all I said. I then called Esha and, like always, she didn't take the call. Slightly frustrated, I called Aditi. She disconnected the call, but was kind enough to send a message on Facebook – 'Sid coming to the airport. Have to pick him up.' I asked her when she could meet me. She didn't reply and I felt annoyed. Putting her aside quickly, I called Smita, but then, she too was busy attending a parent-teacher meeting at her children's school. I sighed in disgust. I didn't have the least inclination to call Preeti. She would of course have spoken to me, but would have added to my frustration, by nagging me to be her boyfriend, to love her like her friends' boyfriends did, and to marry her soon. It was the last thing I wanted at the moment.

I slumped on the beanbag again as my ego had taken a hit. I wondered whether I had used the women or the women had used me. Where are they now when I really need them? What do I mean to them? Was I just an object of pleasure? Was I always a second priority to them? Or had I been one at all in the first place?

Questions darted in my brain left and right, and after a very long time I felt like a loser once again. I was slowly about to slip into a world of empty thoughts and numbness.

But then, I thought of Anjali and called her right away. I somehow recalled that she had important practicals to attend to and I didn't feel like disturbing her. So I disconnected the call before she took it. She called me back instantly. I don't know why, but I didn't pick it up. She called me three more times before giving up eventually.

Myriad thoughts filled my brain and it was distressing to say the least. I kept thinking and didn't even realize when I dozed off.

When I woke up after an hour or so, I saw a message on my phone. It was from Aditi. Apparently, Siddharth's flight had got delayed and Aditi wanted to meet me meanwhile. I felt like a scumbag as I understood clearly that I would remain second priority to her. It had always been that way.

If I were feeling normal, I would probably not have met her, to satisfy my ego and retain my illusory self-respect. But I wasn't at my best. I was feeling weak and submissive. I wanted company. So I asked her to come over, without thinking much.

Needless to say, we had steamy hot sex and it was a great stress-buster as long as it was going on. But soon after I came, the void inside my heart grew wider and bigger. The crazy hormones had filled it only momentarily. I wanted to be left alone. Aditi was cuddling me and was saying something, but I was least interested. Even pretending to listen was becoming difficult. I wished she would understand that I wanted her to stay quiet. But she continued blabbering and uttered something that touched the deepest part of my ego. She had probably spoken the truth and had articulated my real problem, but it felt like everything inside me crumbled in an instant. And then, just like that, I did something that was so unlike me.

'I have fucked you enough. Now you can fuck off!' I said furiously, as I pushed her away from the bed.

'You are such an asshole!' she said, looking angrily at me as she stood up. Her cheeks were red with anger.

I saw her as she stood naked, with her hands on her hips. She was expecting me to say something, but I didn't. It simply doubled her anger.

'All you guys are the same. *You* want women only for sex,' she stated furiously, pointing a finger at me.

I could have refuted her point easily and proved that she was being a hypocrite, given the fact that she had a boyfriend and yet she had slept with me a few moments ago. But I didn't bother to respond and I just looked away from her. Disgusted, she let out a deep sigh and began picking up her undergarments, which were lying on the floor and started wearing them hurriedly. She moved towards the door where her black denims and purple tee were. She wore them in an instant and fished for her comb in her handbag. She brushed her hair and then wore the earrings I had removed before kissing her ears. She took some more time to get ready, gazing at herself in the mirror and adjusting everything, and I wondered how girls gave so much importance to their looks even during moments of distress.

Eventually, before leaving, she threw me a disgusting look and said, 'I will never see your face again.'

'Thank you. Now get lost,' I said as she slammed the door shut.

After she left, I pondered over what had just happened and what had been happening in my life. 'You shouldn't have been so harsh on her' – a soft voice from inside my heart said. But I strangulated it in an instant. I had lost enough in my life by listening to my heart.

Just a few moments ago, I was rolling in bed with Aditi, and after we came together, she began talking to me endlessly, like most girls do after sex. I was more interested in looking at the fan on the ceiling and wondering why it was spinning anticlockwise and not clockwise.

While talking, she had grazed her finger over my shoulder and moved it slowly towards my arms and said, 'Behind these strong muscles, there is a weak heart, yearning to be loved and dying to be cared for. You can hide your pain from the world, Arjun, but not from me.'

That was when I had pushed her from my bed and I didn't really understand why I had reacted so strongly. Was it because I had been hiding my true face from the world successfully all the while? No one had ever tapped the underlying guy inside me, except Krish. But when Aditi said those words, I became very defensive. The last thing I wanted was someone knowing about the void inside me.

I got up, splashed water on my face and looked at myself in the mirror. My eyes were crimson red. And even though I was nowhere near smiling, I saw an evil grin on my face. I splashed water once again and looked at myself. The grin grew wider and scarier. 'How had I been and what have I become?' I asked myself. I saw the image in the mirror once again. I couldn't look at it and smashed the mirror with my hand. Pieces of glass got stuck on my knuckles. A big piece made a deep gash, but it didn't hurt as much as the scars on my heart did.

I then riffled through the shelves to find weed – my temporary solution to permanent problems. I rolled a joint hastily and lighted it. After a few puffs, I felt feather-light and forgot everything that had been going on in my mind. Surreal images flashed in front of my eyes, and when I closed them, I saw myself waiting at the gates of heaven, even though I was, in fact, right in front of my bathroom door.

I tried to get in as I had to pee, but I tripped and fell on my face, my forehead hitting the tap find. The thud sound was what I remembered last, and I woke up to see myself lying on a hospital bed the next morning, with Anjali standing beside me.

■

I tried to sit up, but couldn't without Anjali's help. She put a pillow behind my back. I looked around, trying to recollect how I had ended up in the hospital, but I couldn't recall anything. Anjali saw my predicament. She told me that she got worried when I didn't answer her calls and she came to my room, only to see me lying unconscious in the bathroom. It was she who had brought me to the hospital.

I wanted to thank her, but I didn't. I mean, thanks would be such a small word to express my gratitude to her. She had always been there for me, every time I needed her. I wondered how many people in this world were blessed to have a friend like her. In the dictionary of my life, she was the meaning of the word 'friend'.

I asked her about her practical exams and she tried to change the subject. When I insisted, she said that the exam was the next day and she had already prepared for it. I knew she was lying and asked her to go back to the hostel and study. But she didn't pay heed to my words and chose to stay by my side. I remained silent, lost in my thoughts.

The doctor came late in the evening and said that I could be discharged. Thankfully, the injury was only superficial and there was no internal bleeding. He instructed Anjali to take care of me for a few days.

I touched the bandage on my head and felt acute pain. I was still feeling dizzy. Placing my arm around her shoulder, Anjali helped me walk till the parking lot and made me sit in her car. She drove me to my room and helped me sit on my bed. I was feeling tired and leaned against the wall.

Anjali brought a glass of water mixed with Glucon-D. I drank it and felt somewhat energized. She sat beside me and held my hand with both her hands, trying to comfort me. I rested my head on her shoulder for some emotional support.

After a while, Anjali asked me if I felt okay. I didn't reply. She remained silent and then asked me if it was my parents' memories that disturbed me. She had remembered the date.

I said yes and began telling her how much I had missed my parents in the morning. I craved for their love and affection. I wanted them back in my life even though I knew it was impossible.

Anjali listened to me patiently and I began to feel somewhat better. But truth be told, it wasn't my parents' demise that was really bothering me. It was only a side-effect. The real issue was the bottomless abyss of emptiness in my heart and the meandering thoughts and the endless questions that came with it. I wanted to know the answers as to why I wasn't happy and what was actually missing in my life.

Anjali sensed it and she asked me if there was something else that was bothering me.

For a moment, I wondered how effortlessly she could guess what was going on in my mind. Tears slid from my eyes onto my cheeks and fell on Anjali's hands. She became concerned and asked me to share my pain with her.

I was feeling exhausted because of both physical tiredness and mental stress. So I lay down on the bed, resting my head in Anjali's lap. Anjali began ruffling my hair slowly and I broke into tears and started telling her all that had happened in the past one year.

I told her everything – about Ruchika, Esha, Aditi, Smita, and Preeti. Midway, she stopped caressing me, but her fingers were still entangled in my hair. The fucked-up things that I had done with those women must have definitely shocked her. But I wanted to share it all with someone right then, and who else could I talk to, other than Krish and Anjali?

For about an hour, I went on talking about the immoral life I had led and the strange void that had been torturing me for the past one month. At the end, I felt a huge sense of relief, as if a thousand-kilo stone had been removed from my heart. In Anjali's lap, I found peace and tranquillity, which had been missing in my life.

Anjali remained silent for a while. Her opinion about me would have changed forever. The Arjun who was talking to her wasn't the Arjun she had known since her childhood. She would have definitely felt disappointed with what I had turned myself into. For once, I wondered if she would judge me and begin hating me. I was also scared that she wouldn't be with me the way she had been all along.

But all my fears vanished in no time. It was Anjali, not anyone else. She never judged me, no matter what. Even if the entire world went against me, Anjali would still stand beside me and defend me to death. I didn't know why and I wondered if I really deserved so much affection.

Anjali spoke after a while and reinforced my belief. She said, 'I knew you were up to something and were hiding something from me for the past few months. But I found you happy for most of the year and it was all that mattered to me.'

I felt guilty after hearing her words. I didn't say anything, but the tears that flowed from my eyes said everything.

She continued ruffling my hair and said, 'I am happy now that you have shared everything with me. I hope it made you feel better.'

'It has,' I said, fighting my tears.

She wiped them with her hand and said, 'Don't worry. Give time some time. Everything will be okay.' Her soothing words calmed me down and the river of tears turned into a thin stream. Anjali's lap was wet with my tears, but she didn't move at all.

With one hand, she continued playing with my hair, which had a soothing effect on me. With the other hand, she began tapping my shoulder rhythmically, like mothers do to their kids while singing a lullaby.

'Don't trouble your mind with too many thoughts now. The doctor has advised you to take rest. Just sleep now,' she said.

I closed my eyes and tried to sleep. Anjali continued patting me. Maybe it was because I was sleeping in Anjali's lap, maybe it was her soothing words, or maybe because I could finally share everything with her, I felt a sense of serenity and extreme calmness.

After about an hour or so, I felt a kiss on my forehead. I didn't open my eyes. Anjali might have thought that I was asleep. I felt the peck again. I pretended to be asleep. But I was surprised.

Anjali had kissed my forehead twice!

I didn't know how to react, so I chose not to react at all. I pretended to be asleep as she kissed my cheek. I kept thinking about it for a while with closed eyes, but since I was feeling tired, I slipped into deep sleep soon after. I woke up in the morning and realized that my head was still in Anjali's lap. She was sleeping, leaning against the wall.

All night, she had sat on the bed, nursing me in her lap.

She woke up as soon as I got up. A tsunami of gratitude engulfed my heart. I felt extremely lucky to have someone who cared so much for me.

Anjali got up from the bed and asked me to take it easy. I lay there as she freshened up and made hot coffee for me. I was still feeling slightly dizzy, but felt better after having the coffee. Anjali sat by my side for some time and then prepared to leave as she had to attend the exam. I wished her all the best and said goodbye, though I didn't want her to leave me.

■

For the next one week, I barely spoke to anyone but Krish and Anjali. I wasn't sad or depressed, but I preferred being silent and calm. Ruchika, Esha, and Aditi never really called me during the week. Smita did ask me what had happened, but I started behaving piously with her. The affair was going to end anyway; I could sense her guilt. We behaved like colleagues and nothing else, even though the transition was awkward and quite difficult.

I started focusing on writing lyrics for the feature film. It gave me some solace. But as I wrote the song, I realized my own predicament in life. I understood that I had done much to please my body and ego. And in that process, I had never really cared about what my soul wanted. I was still clueless, but maybe if I had given it a thought, things wouldn't have turned out so bad. My thoughts were my enemy and the void was what empowered those thoughts.

But things were slowly getting better as I got used to living with the questions. Time is powerful and it has its own style of revealing life's answers. I began spending a lot of time with Anjali and it felt so much better than romping with women in bed.

My life fell into a routine and I was content with it. I wished the routine would continue for a few months as, for some reason,

I wanted to stay away from excitement and live a peaceful life. But very soon, I realized that whether we like it or not, life never stays the same. It's like a moving river and changes happen sooner than we want them to.

■

One Friday night, Krish called me over to his place. When I got there, there was a carton of beer on the table. Krish was relaxing on the bed and looking at a picture of some girl on Facebook. We went downstairs, placed the carton in the backseat of his car, and went for a drive. We stopped somewhere and sat on an elevated footpath with the carton beside us. Krish opened a bottle of beer with his teeth, gave it to me, and opened another one for himself.

Silence pervaded between us as we enjoyed our chilled beer.

Krish said calmly in his deep voice, 'I'll be leaving India soon.'

'What?' I said, totally surprised, if not shocked.

'Yes, I've got an on-site opportunity and will be leaving for the USA next Thursday,' he said.

'Well ...'

I didn't know what to say. On the one hand, I was happy that Krish had got a golden opportunity to further his career. On the other hand, I was sad because I was going to lose my best friend. But my happiness for him outweighed my sadness.

'Are you busy this weekend?' Krish said.

'Not really,' I said.

'Well, in that case, I need your help for shopping. Will you?'

'Of course, I will. Anything for you, dude!'

We clinked bottles and gulped the entire beer in one go. We drank the remaining bottles and returned to Krish's home.

The next week was spent shopping and since it was a guy's shopping, we finished everything in no time.

The secret of happiness

Next Thursday, I took the day off from work and went to Krish's room. We packed the luggage together and checked off the items on the list. The flight was supposed to leave at midnight, so we started for the airport in the evening.

Krish was wearing a black round-neck t-shirt and torn jeans. Surprisingly, it was a plain tee with nothing written on the front. He drove the car and we talked on the way. Or rather I talked and Krish just listened to me. His demeanour was unconvincingly calm.

Since he was going to start a new life in a foreign country, I guessed that a lot of things must be running in his mind. So, after a while, I stopped talking and switched on the music system. The Backstreet Boys song *Never Gone* was playing – *Never gone, never far, In my heart is where you are* – and I hummed along, but Krish suddenly stopped the music and played another song. I asked him why he had changed the song, but he didn't reply.

We reached the airport after like an hour, thanks to the traffic in Bangalore. After parking the car, we headed towards the check-in counter. The flight was delayed by two hours, so we sat in the lobby, sipping cold coffee.

'Exactly four years ago, this day, she left me,' Krish said.

'Who?' I was confused.

'Pooja,' he said.

I thought for a while trying to access the database of Krish's girlfriends. I didn't remember all the names, but I was sure that Pooja wasn't on that list.

'Who's Pooja?' I asked inquisitively.

'The love of my life,' he said and his voice quivered.

I was surprised. I put my hand on his shoulder and bent my head a little towards him. He turned towards me and his eyes were welling with tears.

WTF!I couldn't believe it – Krish was crying?!! 'Wait a minute! This can't be real,' I said to myself as it took some time for me to digest that *even* Krish could cry. That behind this happy-go-lucky Krish could be a guy who would burst into tears. And that too for a girl!

'I know what you must be thinking, that how can Krish – a guy who changes girlfriends every other month – shed tears for a girl,' he said reading my mind.

I was confused.

'Well, I wasn't always like this, Arjun. I loved a girl in college – truly, madly, deeply. She meant the world to me then. I proposed to her in the beginning of the first year of college. And on the last day of first year, she said yes. She kissed me on the lips that day and I can still feel the softness of her lips on mine.

'The very next day, we were together all day. We spoke about our dreams, fears, and lives. We promised each other that we would stay together forever, no matter what. She hugged me tightly before I was about to leave and I kissed her on the forehead.

'The next three years of college were the most beautiful days of my life. I used to look forward to seeing her every day. We would spend almost all the time together, holding each other's hands, teasing each other, whispering sweet nothings, and making love every once in a while. Our love grew with time and we became inseparable.

'College ended before we knew it. I got a job in Deloitte and she in Cognizant. We were quite happy. We were planning to get married after two years, as we felt that we needed to focus on our careers first. But Pooja's parents started forcing her to get married. She tried to convince them to wait for two more years, but they were adamant and would blackmail her emotionally every day.

'So, we devised a plan to solve the problem – she would go for her Master's to the US, as it would take about two years for her to finish graduation. By that time, I would get settled as well and we could then marry happily. She disagreed initially as she didn't want to stay away from me at all, but agreed eventually for the sake of our greater good. "We will anyway live the rest of our life together. It's just a matter of two years," I would say. Her mom was sceptical, but her dad was okay with her going abroad for studies, provided she would come back after two years and get married.

'The day finally came when she had to leave for the US. The separation was painful and she was in tears. Even I was crying, but on the inside. I needed to be strong.

'We hugged each other for a very long time and kissed goodbye.

'The first two months in the US were very difficult for her. She would call me and cry every day. It was hard for me to console her, but thanks to Skype, we would video-chat almost every day and send virtual kisses to each other.

'I felt she was feeling lonely and so I introduced her to a senior of mine who was doing MS in the same college. He asked me not to worry, that he would take care of her. They hit it off well and I was happy as I didn't have to worry much about her. But little did I know that my worries were only going to begin.

'I didn't expect it to happen, but gradually the frequency of our calls decreased. She would barely message me and we would Skype only once a week. She would say she'd been busy with her coursework and I was somewhat okay with it. But I began missing her badly.

'A few weeks later, when we Skyped, both Pooja and the guy were present in her room. Any idiot could figure out that they had grown very comfortable with each other. She seemed very happy too. The guy thanked me for introducing Pooja to him and flashed a sinister smile in the end. A surge of jealousy rose within me and I was on the brink of going crazy. I wished I could go to the US right away.

'After a while, she said that she had to go for class and would speak to me later. She blew me a flying kiss and closed the laptop lid, without disconnecting the call. I just sat there in front of my laptop watching the black screen which had been filled with her beautiful face a few moments ago. I looked at the screen for some more time imagining Pooja talking to me and saying she was missing me badly. And as I was about to get up from the chair, I heard the sounds of muffled voices. I was confused initially, but it didn't take me much time to realize that the voices belonged to Pooja and my senior.

'I increased the volume of the speakers and what I heard destroyed my faith in love forever. I could hear them kissing each other, which was followed by her soft moans. The guy said that she looked sexy in her outfit and she said that she'd look sexier without it. A few more sweet nothings between them followed and I couldn't take it anymore. I smashed my laptop in fury and stormed out of my house, and sat on a pavement. It started pouring, and my tears got mixed with the rain.

'I was totally devastated and didn't know what to do. Though I was very furious, I chose not to lose my cool. I wanted to deal with the situation carefully.

'The next time we had a video chat, she acted normally, as if nothing was going on between her and the senior. She didn't talk to me for long. Though she said she missed me and all, it was clear from her tone that she didn't really mean it.

'Over the next few days, she almost stopped messaging me and her messages became curt too. Sometimes she would pick fights with me for no reason and wouldn't answer my calls at all.

'I could understand that she was trying to ignore me, maybe because she had started liking that guy or she didn't really need me in her life anymore. But I loved her to bits and couldn't imagine life without her.

'Over a period of time, I became more and more subdued, until one day I couldn't take it anymore.

'I was drunk that day and she picked up a fight with me, again for a silly reason. I shouted at her and said that she was a bitch who was two-timing. And that's it! Just like that, everything between us was over.

'"How could you call me a bitch?" she said and disconnected the call.

'I tried calling her multiple times, but she didn't answer. My messages went unanswered. I sent her long, apologetic emails but she didn't respond. One day when I called her for like forty times, she answered and said harshly, "Don't irritate me. I don't love you anymore. I can't love a guy who calls me a bitch and who doesn't trust me. And please don't call me again."

'I really wanted to talk to her again and I'd die a thousand deaths just to hear her voice. But I never called her again, hoping she would miss me and call me. But she didn't and it dawned upon me that the happiest days of my life had just got over.

'I moved to Bangalore then and was in a similar position like you were when we first met. Pooja and that guy got married later. No prizes for guessing that she didn't invite me to her wedding, but I went in disguise, unable to contain the urge to look at the love of my life.

'She looked beautiful and happy. And for some strange reason, I wasn't really angry with her. I loved her to the moon and back, and though it might sound foolish, I still love her more than anything else in this world.

'After that, like you, I became a Devdas for a few months. And to overcome the sorrow, I started reinventing myself completely and turned into a flirt. I felt good initially and I loved it when I could make girls throw themselves at me, but as time passed, no matter how many beautiful girls I fucked, I couldn't get even an iota of happiness that I used to get in just being with Pooja. I tried my best to forget her, but I could never really move on. She is still there in some corner of my heart. And I don't think I will be able to forget her until my last breath.' Krish ended his monologue and sighed heavily.

I was dumbstruck, to say the least. My dad used to say that behind every person there lies a story which makes them what they are. Many a time, the story isn't known to anybody. I had been with Krish for more than a year and hadn't got even a hint of all this. He was always cheerful and lived life to the fullest, trying his best to bring joy in the lives of people around him. But at that moment, I realized that people can be totally empty deep inside and yet be very cheerful on the outside.

I didn't know what to say to Krish. If there is one thing guys are very bad at, it's comforting other guys during emotional moments. Women would have instinctively known what to do. All I could manage was to pat him on his shoulder and say, 'She lost an amazing guy.'

He wiped his tears, cleared his throat, and said, 'I never shared this with anyone. It's just that I needed to get it out of my system.' He said after a small pause, 'Nevertheless, before I leave for the US, I want to tell you something.'

'Please,' I said and prepared to listen to him intently.

'Philosophical as it may sound, but we are the sum total of three components – body, ego, and soul. Your body always craves for relaxation. Your ego craves for pleasure. But your soul ... all it wants is to be happy.'

I wondered where he was heading.

He continued, 'Lust satisfies the needs of your body and ego, but it does nothing for your soul, because your soul is nourished by the pristine happiness that comes with pure love.'

'Hmm.'

'And trying to find happiness through lust is like trying to fill water in a bottle with holes at the bottom. The bottle may appear full for a while but it gets empty eventually. Likewise, lust gives pleasure to your heart momentarily but leaves you with a void in the end. And the only way to fill that void is through unconditional love. Nothing else can keep your heart at peace.'

Listening to Krish at that moment felt like reading a Paulo Coelho novel.

He continued in his deep voice, 'In this life, if you're lucky enough, you'll find a girl that your heart truly loves. And by any chance, if she loves you more than you love her, make her yours for life. Trust me, buddy, that's the single greatest secret of happiness – spending a lifetime with *the one.*'

I found the statement very profound and it reminded me of Anjali. He continued, 'When you came to Bangalore heartbroken, I encouraged you to become a flirt, because I didn't want you to remain a loser all your life. Life has to be lived fully, experiencing pleasure until you find happiness. It's tricky, but in many cases, it's only after men experience the pleasures of lust at its fullest that they begin to appreciate love at its best. Now you know that better.'

He said that and forced himself to smile. I smiled in return, but my mind was busy registering what he had just said. We sat in silence for the next few minutes.

Soon, it was time for him to leave. We shook hands, hugged each other, and said our goodbyes. Before leaving, he handed me a piece of paper, saying that the lines on the paper summed up everything that he wanted to say. He said that the lyrics of a Hindi song were his gift to his favourite lyricist. He then ruffled my hair, wished me all the best, and walked towards the check-in counter.

I opened the paper and began reading:

Chaahe jo tumhe pure dil se,
Milta hai woh mushkil se.
Aisa jo koi kahin hai,
Bas wohi sabse haseen hai.
Us haath ko tum thaamlo,
Woh meherbaan kal ho na ho.

I looked up and saw Krish walking away. That's when I noticed the back of his T-shirt. It said, 'Of all the lies she told me, "I love you" was the sweetest.'

He didn't turn back and I knew that I wouldn't see him again in a long time.

I drove back home, all the while pondering about what Krish had said, especially about finding *the one*. I was also surprised that Anjali had come to my mind as soon as he had said that. I wanted to call her that very instant, but then saw it was past 1 a.m. I put my phone back into my pocket. By the time I reached my room, I was dog-tired and slumped on the bed.

The next day, I reached office early as I had to finish some pending work. Soon, I felt a hand on my shoulder. I turned around to find Sanjay standing there.

He had a big smile plastered on his face. He sat on the desk, dangling his legs, and said, 'This evening, cancel any appointments that you have. I am throwing a party.'

'But sir ...'

In spite of his insistence to call him by his name and not address him as sir, I still called him sir, out of admiration and respect, if nothing else.

'No ifs and buts. You are coming. And you don't say no to your manager when he wants to throw a party.' He winked and left.

Quite frankly, I would have had no problem going to the party, but for the void inside me. I had no other option but to say yes to him.

I spent most of the day at my desk, finishing my work. In the evening, Sanjay asked me to go along with him in his BMW.

The entire team under Sanjay went to a five-star hotel at around 7 p.m. The bar in the hotel was dimly lit and had an amazing ambience. Glass tables, with beanbags around them, were scattered across the floor. A local band was performing songs requested by the audience. The girl who was singing wore a short skirt and had smooth legs. And a smoother voice. The guy with her had long hair and a short beard. They looked like future rockstars.

We occupied six tables and my colleagues began ordering whisky, brandy, Scotch and wine. Others ordered fresh lime juice and were quite content with that. Alcohol filled up the glasses on the tables slowly and was emptied into stomachs gradually.

After some time, everyone was less inhibited and more relaxed. Sanjay took five rounds of Scotch and I felt it was a little too much for him. His speech became slightly slurred and he began talking about his expeditions in various countries during his younger days. He had seen almost the whole of Europe. Then, he took another shot and went on the stage.

He whispered something in the singer's ears. The singer smiled and moved away. Sanjay took the mike and began singing an old Hindi song and the band played the music accordingly.

Tere bina zindagi se koi shikwa toh nahi,
shikwa nahi, shikwa nahi, shikwa nahi.
Tere bina zindagi bhi lekin, zindagi toh nahi,
zindagi nahi, zindagi nahi, zindagi nahi

When he had finished singing, everyone in our team clapped – a few because they liked Sanjay's singing and others simply because he was the manager. He raised both his hands to acknowledge the appreciation and walked back to his seat. In that dim light, I noticed his eyes becoming moist. But the moisture lasted less than a second. Sanjay was back to regaling us with tales of his bachelor days.

Alcohol continued to flow and so did the conversation. But after about two hours, people began leaving slowly. I stayed as I had no one waiting for me except my bed.

For some reason, that day, Sanjay continued to drink, until only the two of us remained.

'Sir, it's quite late and you are drunk way beyond limits,' I said in a low voice.

'Yeah. I should stop,' he said and turned to the waiter. 'Waiter! One more drink.'

I couldn't stop him from having another drink, but he promised it would be the last for the day. He gave his credit card to pay the bill. He was too drunk to sign the merchant copy of the bill and so I signed on his behalf. The waiter didn't bother.

I tried putting Sanjay's arm around my shoulder to make sure he didn't stumble along our way to the parking lot. But he removed my hand and tried walking on his own. After two steps, he tripped, and he was about to fall down, but I held him at the very last moment.

The next minute, he threw up. It was pretty much expected. He began cleaning his face with his T-shirt – a sight to behold. He came to his senses, somewhat. He went to the washroom to clean himself and I went to fetch some water, lemon, and buttermilk.

Sanjay was in a much better state after that. I thought it would be wise to just sit down for a while before we headed back home. So we chose to sit on the manicured lawn within the premises of the hotel.

Sanjay sat cross-legged, silently, for a few minutes, deeply engrossed in thought. After a few minutes, he covered his face with his hands and began sobbing.

WTF! Wait a minute! Just a day ago, I had seen the super cool Krish in tears. And now this rock-star manager.

What are these cool men made of? I asked myself.

'Sir,' I said, patting his shoulder slowly.

He lifted his head and said, 'Today is her birthday.'

'Whose birthday, sir?'

'Aarti's.'

I knew Aarti was Sanjay's six-year-old daughter. But I couldn't understand why Sanjay was sobbing on his daughter's birthday.

'Sir, why are you so upset on your daughter's birthday? Is everything okay?'

He looked at me and said, 'It's not my daughter's birthday.'

'Well ...then ...'

'Aarti... my first love.'

Oh fuck! I guess I already knew what Sanjay was going to say – another tragic love story where the guy is still unable to forget the girl. But I didn't say anything and he continued.

'Aarti and I knew each other even before we knew the difference between a boy and a girl. We went to the same school and same tuition classes and spent most of the time together. Best friends. And then we fell in love in our adolescence.

'She was very nice, affectionate, caring, and beautiful. She loved me almost as much as my mother did. I loved her too, but not as much as she did. But we were happy together.

'But over a period of time, I began to understand the world better and desired to achieve something big in life. I wanted to travel round the world, meet lots of people, and explore life. I was becoming ambitious and wanted to become a great person. After weighing my options, education in the USA seemed the right option.

'But Aarti wasn't ambitious. Though she wanted to take up a job, she was more into getting married to me and taking care of our kids and having a blissful family life. She wanted a husband who would do a day job, come back home, and spend time with the family.

'As time passed, I started taking her for granted and spent more time preparing to go to the US. I didn't tell Aarti of my plans. I just didn't know how to tell her. She would cry sometimes and ask why

I was ignoring her. I would console her with excuses and continue with my plans.

'After a few months, my efforts bore fruit and my US visa was approved. I was still unsure about how I would tell this to Aarti.

'And then I did a stupid thing. I decided to go away without telling her. Deep inside, I knew it would hurt her, but I felt she would move on eventually. At least, that's what I thought, but I was only partially right. She did move on, but from earth to heaven,' Sanjay said and paused.

My jaw dropped when I heard the last words. I was speechless. Dumbfounded, to say the least.

He took out an old paper from his pocket. It was a letter written in ink. It was smudged here and there, most probably because of someone's teardrops falling on the paper. I took the letter from him and as soon as I read a few lines, my hands trembled. It's not every day that you hold a suicide note in your hands.

Dear Sanjay,

I hate you, but I love you. You left me all alone. Why did you do that? Couldn't you meet me just once before leaving? I would have kissed you goodbye for one last time and would have happily let you go. You know how much I am hurt, don't you?

I feel my love wasn't sufficient to keep you happy. And so you left. Couldn't you take me with you? I would have left everything for you. You know that, right?

But alas! You are gone now and I am here writing this stupid letter to you, with my eyes welling with tears and my heart devoid of any hope.

I try to convince myself, but my heart keeps asking too many questions. Did you ever really love me? What happened to our promises of living together forever? Didn't you think of me at least once before leaving? Was your love just pretence?

Don't tell me it is even if it is. I don't think I can bear to hear that.

My dear, I am sorry to bother you with these questions. But I won't be troubling you anymore.

I saw my whole life with you, even before I knew anything about love. I loved you more than I loved myself. But now that you are no more in my life, I feel dead inside – completely shattered, hopeless and broken, so much that I just can't take it anymore.

Mumma and Pappa want me to get married to a distant relative. He is a nice guy and he likes me too. I wish I could tell him that my heart, body and soul belong to you. But I am a girl from a conservative family and you know it's almost impossible for me to say that. I never imagined another guy touching even my hand. And now sharing a bed with another guy is way beyond my imagination.

I can't hurt Mumma and Pappa, and I can't hurt myself. And I can't take this pain anymore. I feel like killing this pain this very instant and the only way to do that is to kill myself. I've decided to take leave Sanjay, hoping we would be together at least in our next incarnation.

I wish you all the happiness. Be happy, always. Marry a nice girl who will love you. And I hope all your dreams come true.

Before I say my final goodbye, I just have one wish, Sanjay. One last wish. Please name your daughter Aarti. Would you do that? Is that too much to ask?

Bye forever.

Yours and only yours,
Aarti

I read the letter and a strange kind of sadness filled my heart. I felt sorry for Aarti.

Sanjay took the letter from my hands, folded it neatly and put it back in his pocket. Silence pervaded between us for a few minutes.

He regained his composure and started speaking words of wisdom. His voice was deep and profound, just like Krish's the previous day.

He said, 'I was a fool to let go of her. After leaving her, I went to the US, studied well, and worked for various multinational companies at various positions. I travelled around the world and by the time I was thirty years old, I made almost all my dreams come true. But there was always a void in my life. I tried to dodge it for a few years, but succumbed to it eventually. The void was, invariably, Aarti.

'Now I realize that though my dreams satisfied my ego, they didn't really give me happiness. I was truly happy when I was being my true self with Aarti. When I came back to India, my dad handed me the suicide note and I was devastated. It was the most horrible moment of my life. A little voice inside my head said that she didn't commit suicide. I murdered her.'

I had never seen Sanjay in this state of mind. I didn't know what to do or say, except listen to his words silently.

He continued, 'I then tried my best to forget her, but I couldn't. My parents got me married and I played the role of a husband well. My wife is a good woman, but I could never really love her like I loved Aarti.

'The only thing I could do for Aarti was name my daughter after her. I hope she will forgive me for my misdeed.'

He stopped and it was my turn to say something.

'Sir, everybody makes mistakes. There's no point in you killing yourself for something that happened a long time ago,' I said.

'That's true, but logic rarely wins over emotions,' he said and continued, 'There is something that I want to tell you, out of my experience. I hope I don't sound preachy.'

'Please go ahead, sir.'

'Okay, then listen. In this life, if you're lucky enough, you'll find a girl that your heart truly loves. And by any chance, if she loves you more than you love her, make her yours for life. Trust me, Arjun, that's the single greatest secret of happiness – spending a lifetime with *the one*.'

I opened my mouth in amazement. It was déjà vu. Those were the exact words that Krish had told me.

'What happened?' Sanjay said.

'Nothing sir. It's just that … nothing really.'

Sanjay didn't bother to ask. We sat there for a few more minutes and then decided to leave. I drove the car while Sanjay slept blissfully in the back seat. A million thoughts started running in my mind and I was completely lost in those thoughts, so much that I didn't even remember the road I took to my home.

When I reached my room, I helped Sanjay out of the car and carefully settled him on my bed. I took a bedsheet and a pillow and went upstairs. I lay down on the terrace, watching the sky and twinkling stars.

I began to wonder how much Krish and Sanjay had suffered, how much they had loved, and how amazingly they had hidden all the pain deep inside their hearts.

Is everyone in this world like that, suffering from some kind of pain silently? Do we really need that someone who completes us? Is the pleasure of lust trivial before the happiness of love? Why is it that everyone craves for unconditional love in spite of all the worldly pleasures they can get?

As if these questions were not enough, a few more questions bogged my mind and kept troubling me.

Is there any point in living a life without *the one*? Am I secretly seeking love? Did I really love anyone truly?

Finding Juliet

As my mind was busy dealing with myriad questions, I began to see a silhouette on the moon. It slowly grew brighter and damn ... it was Anjali! I saw her beautiful face, pretty eyes, and windblown hair. She was looking at me. A smile flashed on my face automatically. But it didn't last long.

Her senior Rahul came into the picture. He held her hand and they exchanged rings. My eyebrows drew together in a frown of disbelief. She looked quite happy with him. They started walking away after kissing each other and she waved me goodbye before leaving. And then the clouds covered the moon.

I woke up drenched in sweat. And felt sharp pangs of pain in my chest. I saw the moon again. It was full and white, but there was no one there.

Maybe it was a sign from God, I felt – that I'd feel like crap if I let go of Anjali from my life. I remembered Krish's and Sanjay's words about love. It suddenly dawned on me that Anjali was *the girl*. She was *the one*. She was *my love*.

'Damn! Why didn't I realize this all this while? Such a fool I am!' I said, hitting myself on my forehead.

It didn't take me long to understand that I'd be extremely happy if I lived my entire life with her. There was no doubt about it.

I recollected all the moments I had spent with her and the times she had been there for me. She had loved me dearly and I always took her for granted.

Now that I had finally realized my folly and was clear about what I really wanted, I felt like telling her right away. I could have waited till morning, but a strange fear gripped me as I wondered if it would be too late. So without wasting any time, I started running towards her hostel. 'The best time to profess one's love is *now*', some wise man had said.

I could have gone to her hostel in Sanjay's car or on my bike. But I was so exhilarated that I just ran like Milkha Singh all the way. Her hostel was a few kilometres away and I reached there in twenty-five minutes, panting heavily.

It was 1.30 a.m. and the hostel gates were closed. The watchman was, luckily, snoring. I thought of calling her but, in my excitement, I had forgotten my phone in my room. But wait, I knew her room number.

Slyly, I jumped the walls and entered the girls' hostel. Almost everyone was asleep, except a few students who were sitting in their rooms studying. Luckily, no one was in the corridor. I found Anjali's room and knocked on the door. She opened it yawning, but was shocked beyond belief when she saw me. Before she could squeak, I closed her mouth with my hand and entered the room.

'What are *you* doing here?' she asked as I removed my hand from her mouth.

'I came here to tell you something.'

'Couldn't you ...'

'I couldn't wait till morning,' I said and looked deep into her eyes. We fell silent but our eyes were still talking. I don't know why my eyes became a little moist and her eyes became kind. My eyes were filled with love and her eyes were filled with contentment.

She understood everything, I guess. One look told her everything, I felt. Girls are pretty good at this. You don't really have to tell them everything. If they know you, they just understand, without you even saying a single word.

'Anjali, I...'

'Shhh...' She put her finger on my lips and said, 'Not now. We will meet tomorrow evening at the old bench near the lake.'

'But ...'

'Nothing doing.'

'But just listen...'

'Will you leave now or should I call the watchman?' she said in mock anger, stifling her smile.

I didn't have much choice. So I left silently. To my horror, the watchman caught me while leaving. I tried to convince him with some cock-and-bull story, but he got into an altercation with me. For fifteen minutes, he tortured me and even threatened to call the police. And as soon as I heard the word police, I became pretty sure that I would land in jail the next day. I even feared newspapers splashing news about a software engineer caught trespassing in a girls' hostel. How embarrassing it would be! But luckily, Anjali saw me through the window and came to my rescue. She spoke to the watchman and he let me go.

'Thank God you came to help me. Or else I don't know what would have happened,' I said.

'I was watching the entire scene from my window,' she said and began laughing uncontrollably, clutching her stomach.

'It's not funny. You should have come here at the very beginning then,' I said, trying to be angry.

'Watchman!' she shouted.

I closed her mouth with my hand and said, 'Okay, okay, I am leaving.'

'That's like a good boy,' she said coyly and left.

Girls, I tell you, love drama so much, especially when they know that you like them.

I went back to my room, walking all the way to BTM Layout, kicking a few pebbles along the way. By the time I reached, it was almost three o' clock. I tried to sleep, but couldn't. I took out my phone and began looking at Anjali's pics. Now that I knew I was in love with her, she looked much cuter. After some time, I put my phone away and closed my eyes. I began to see her again, now in my imagination. I was tense. Something was eating my heart out. I wanted the next day to come as soon as possible.

Realizing the futility of my efforts to sleep, I picked up a pen and paper and began writing down my feelings. I had never in my life prepared my thoughts before speaking to Anjali, but now I was worried as to what I'd tell her the next day. They say with girls it's all about saying the right things at the right time. After about a million papers thrown into the dustbin, I finally wrote something worthy. I read it once and almost memorized it. After thinking for two more hours about the next day's meet, I don't remember when I fell asleep.

I woke up late the next day, and saw that Sanjay had already left. He had left a small note saying 'Thank You!' So I had brunch, and slept till late afternoon. The alarm clock woke me up and, for the first time in my life, I took a long time to get ready. I had never given much thought to my appearance when I was to meet Anjali. But this time, it was going to be different. This moment would last for a lifetime and I wanted to make it special. I thought of all the ways to make the moment memorable.

I wore a brand new white shirt and blue denims. I tucked my shirt and wore a brown leather belt. Not to brag, but I looked quite handsome. I set my hair and sprayed on a bit of the perfume that Anjali had gifted me. Finally, after wearing casual brown shoes, I left for her hostel. The place where she wanted to meet was nearby.

On the way, I went to a jewellery shop to buy a ring. I looked at gold rings first, but felt that gold was unlucky for me, recollecting the bad experience I had had with Neha. So I bought a platinum ring this time, with an 'A' engraved inside a heart. It looked far more beautiful and I imagined Anjali wearing it and going 'Awww!'

Then I went to an Archies shop and bought a cute big brown teddy bear. I wanted her to hug it every time she missed me. I know I was thinking like a fool again, but what's the point of being in love and not being stupid?

I then bought a few heart-shaped balloons and filled them with air (and love). In the shop, I saw a big greeting card. On the cover, there was a cute picture of a girl and a boy, about five years old, who were holding their hands and walking in the woods. It reminded me of the way Anjali had held my hand for the very first time at the bus stop. I took the card and opened it. It was blank. I borrowed a pen from the shop owner and thought about what I should write in that empty space. I deliberated for ten to fifteen minutes and then wrote only three words – *I love you.*

On the way, I stopped at a florist's. The boy at the counter saw my face and smiled. Maybe he understood from my excitement that I was going to propose to a girl, for he prepared a bouquet of red roses without me even asking for it. It was quite lovely and the little drops of water glistening on the rose petals made it look lovelier. I knew Anjali's fetish for roses and I hoped she'd feel happy to see them. I paid for the flowers and tipped the boy generously.

'All the best, sir!' he beamed and waved.

It was 5 p.m. when I reached Anjali's hostel. I went to that old bench near the lake. She had asked me to wait there.

I sat there for a while and practised the speech that I had prepared the previous night. Thank God I remembered everything, which was unusual, given my miserable memory.

After rehearsing one more time, I got down to decorating the bench. First, I stuck a few coloured papers here and there. On each of them, I stuck a few photographs – most of them were selfies that we had taken over the past few years and a few childhood pics. I then tied most of the heart-shaped balloons around the edges of the bench and a few in the middle, placing the teddy bear in between.

After taking care of all that, I dialled Anjali's number. Her picture flashed on the screen and brought a smile on my face, even though I was tense inside. My heart was pounding as I made the call. Given my experience with girls, I knew that it took no time for them to change their mind. What if she came up with some lame excuse and said we would meet later? All my preparations would go down the drain. Moreover, I didn't want to feel sorry for myself in case I'd been too late in expressing my feelings for her. I didn't want that nightmare to come true – the one where I saw her getting married to that Rahul.

Luckily, she took the call and I heaved a sigh of relief. She said she had been waiting for my call. I felt happy. I guessed she was as excited to meet me as I was to meet her. I beamed with happiness. She said she was almost ready and would come in ten minutes. I just said okay and disconnected the call.

I then waited for her, checking my watch a million times in those ten minutes. For some reason, the clock ticked slowly and during those tense moments, I was able to understand Einstein's theory of relativity better. Ten minutes passed. Then, fifteen minutes passed. Then, half an hour. No sign of Anjali.

Anjali wasn't the kind of girl who took long to get ready. I wanted to call her, but refrained. Maybe she wanted to make me wait. Probably she was taking revenge on me for making her wait all her life. Or maybe I was just thinking way too much. Love does this to people. When in love, almost everyone over-thinks, I guess.

I saw my watch tick one more time and then I turned my head towards the right. And God! What a sight it was! I stood up involuntarily.

Anjali was walking towards me in her characteristic slow gait. With her loose hair rising and falling at every step, it was like watching Sonali Bendre walking in slow motion.

She was wearing a white kurta with transparent short sleeves. The upper half had some beautiful embellishments and the lower part had lovely pleats. Her transparent chunni was beautifully embroidered and her churidar was crinkled at the bottom, just above her anklets. Her strapped sandals were shiny white, matching her dress. Not to mention those dangling earrings with white pearls.

Overall, she looked like an angel minus the halo on her head and wings on her back. I looked at her in amazement. She reached me and snapped her fingers right in front of my face, and I came back to my senses.

She looked at the bench and smiled. She moved the balloons aside and sat on the bench elegantly. She signalled at me to sit beside her. Like a trained robot, I obliged and sat on the bench.

I didn't know where to begin. I saw her manicured hands and couldn't resist holding them. She trembled a bit, but didn't resist. I intertwined my fingers with hers and looked at her. She looked at me and her smile grew wider. I tried to recollect the speech I had prepared the previous day, but my memory failed me. I was so lost in Anjali's beauty that I forgot everything.

'So, you wanted to say something?' Anjali began.

'Well...umm...er...'

She laughed and I gave her an embarrassed smile.

I then did something that was purely instinctive. I knelt down and held both her hands. She moved forward a bit, growing a little uncomfortable. I gestured to her to relax and sit properly. I took out the ring from my pocket and said what I was longing to say – '*I love you*'.

For the first time in my life, I felt I really meant it. I looked into her eyes while saying those three magical words and, in an instant, my eyes became moist. It was like the best thing I had ever done in my life. I felt my heart brimming with love and my mind experiencing peace for the first time. I felt like a prisoner being freed after decades of imprisonment. But the difference was that, here, I was both the prisoner and the prison.

I tried to say something, but everything seemed superfluous. Why is it so difficult to express how much you love someone?

I sat there silently, looking into her eyes. Those eyes were welling with tears and overflowing with excitement. She bit her lips, trying to control her tears, but her emotions were too strong; she started sobbing. She took her hands away from mine to cover her face.

I just knelt there watching her regain her composure slowly. After a while, she held both my hands with one hand and ruffled my hair with the other. She was still silent though.

'Say something.' I paused and said, 'My knees are hurting.' I said it mimicking pain and removing a pebble from underneath my knee.

'Get up, you idiot,' she said instantly and pulled me up.

We stood together, with only inches between us. She wrapped her arms around my neck and sobbed again.

She then said, 'I love you too, stupid. I love you more than anything else in life. I have loved you since forever. Why did you take so long to tell me?' She began hitting me on the chest with both her fists.

I feigned pain in the chest and she stopped. She hugged me again and I put my arms around her, held her tightly, and lifted her in the air.

We sat on the bench again, calmed down.

'Will you marry me, Anjali?' I asked, in Bollywood style.

'Well...I need some time to think about it,' she said coyly. Girls and their drama, I tell you. I sighed helplessly.

'Fine. Take your time,' I said, making a face.

She smiled at my expression, held me by my chin, and kissed me on the cheek. At that instant, I wanted to hold her and kiss her lips. But I didn't. I was beyond happy to get kissed on the cheek. There was an entire lifetime left to kiss her lips.

But Anjali had other plans. She turned my face towards her and brought her face closer. There was a gap of only a few inches between our lips. Our breathing grew heavier, our eyes closed, and the inevitable happened. I felt her soft lips on mine and there were butterflies in my stomach.

What surprised me most was that even though I had kissed many girls before, I had never really felt the joy I was experiencing at that moment. I then realized that a true kiss isn't really coming together of lips, it's actually a meeting of two souls.

I was enjoying the trance as Anjali kept planting baby kisses on my lips. I liked the mushiness and felt a childlike joy inside.

After a while, Anjali suddenly stopped and looked around to see if anyone was watching us. I scanned around too. Confirming that there was no one, we went back to kissing each other again. I usually placed my hands on a girl's waist while kissing, but this time I placed my hands on Anjali's head and caressed her hair softly.

I don't remember for how long we kissed, but I remember that we were almost exhausted. I think there was so much love hidden inside and the kiss served as an outlet.

After we felt content, I looked at Anjali's face. She was feeling shy and was blushing. I tilted my head to make eye contact, but she covered her face with her hands. When I tried to remove them, she suddenly put her arms around my neck and hugged me.

The hug was very tight and I wondered if my bones would break. But I endured it, for love, if nothing else. After a while, I felt my neck becoming wet. It was because of the tears rolling down Anjali's cheeks.

Girls cry a lot, both when they are happy and sad. I was glad that the tears from Anjali's eyes were tears of happiness. Anjali was a strong woman and I had rarely seen her cry. I began wondering how strong she must have been to keep all the love for me inside of her and live in the hope that someday I would love her back. The wait must have been torturous.

As I kept thinking, I wondered how girls can love so unconditionally, in spite of all the flaws in their men. I marvelled at their ability to conceal love, killing themselves on the inside, and yet smiling beautifully on the outside.

My reverie broke as Anjali softened her hug and went back to sitting normally. She was still crying though. I wanted to wipe her tears, but I did something else instead. I kissed her tears and they got absorbed by my lips. They were slightly salty but I didn't mind.

I then kissed her forehead and rested my head on her shoulder, holding her hand in mine. We remained silent and I felt an unusual calmness, like the hurricane inside my head had finally subsided. The dust in my life was now cleared and the path ahead appeared serene and bright. I had never felt this way before. I held Anjali's hand tightly and I don't know why I felt infinitely better.

After some time, we got up as it was late. We began walking together, holding each other's hands and intertwining our fingers. We watched the sun set as a new dawn was about to begin in our lives.

We continued walking together for a while, but suddenly Anjali stopped and pulled her hand away from mine. I had moved two steps ahead of her by then and turned back surprised. She then jumped on my back and put her arms around my neck. It was very childish of her to do that, but I didn't mind.

I stumbled a bit when she jumped, but for the first time in my life, I felt my feet quite stable. She was a bit heavy for me, but for the first time in my life, I felt feather-light. She kissed me on the lips, but for the first time in my life, I felt I was kissed by happiness...